FLIGHT FROM SANCTUARY

STAR MAGE SAGA BOOK 6

J.J. GREEN

1

"And, finally, the time came when our mountain home, which had been our sanctuary for generations, was no longer safe, and we had to flee, taking with us only our most precious items. Some of us brought paper books, though such things were already old and fragile by then, and others took cherished family heirlooms like jewelry, paintings, and handcrafted ornaments. A few wanted to bring animals they'd grown to love, but the Great Mage ruled this out, with no exceptions. The colony ships did not accommodate any living organisms other than humans.

"So those among us who loved their pets and working beasts created clones of them and froze the embryos, then added them to the stock of wild and domesticated animal species. We also collected and loaded seeds and spores of plants—particularly trees, for wood is essential to our way of life. Most important of all, we brought our lore and the history of our kind, written within these pages and held within the minds of the three Spirit Mages."

Nahla paused and frowned, looking up from her screen.

"Go on," said Ferne. He was inside a closet, checking all his things were still there, and he'd stuck out his head to speak. "I want to hear the bit about the fight at the spaceport, when they finally left Earth. That has to be coming soon."

He and the rest of the children had decided to return to the suite on the *Bathsheba* they'd occupied before going into stasis. Carina hadn't lived there, but to her it looked as though the Regians hadn't touched the place. Even so, now that the battle with the aliens to reclaim the colony ship had been won and no other threats were looming, a few missing personal items would have been a small price to pay.

Oriana and Darius were lying on a double bed, Darius resting his head on his sister's lap as they listened to Nahla. Parthenia was messaging someone as she sat at a dressing table. Carina sat on a sofa, working as she waited for Bryce.

Ignoring Ferne's comment, Nahla said to Jace, "I thought there was only ever one Spirit Mage."

The older man was sitting across a single bed, resting his back against the wall, his long legs hanging over the side.

"I've only ever known there to be one," he replied, smoothing the hair of his thick, black beard. "Our old Spirit Mage, Magda, said another of her kind would appear—a child —when she entered the later stages of her life, and she was correct." He smiled at Darius. "Aside from that, she never spoke of other Spirit Mages. What the text says is news to me, but I'm not saying your translation is wrong. I've learned many new things from the ancient documents. I'm impressed by your work. I'd no idea you were so good."

Nahla blushed and lifted her interface a little in an attempt to hide her face.

Carina was deeply impressed by her sister's efforts, too. She'd had no idea Nahla had been reading and translating the copies of the mages' documents in the months before entering Deep Sleep. The young girl was full of surprises, like the time she'd discovered Mezban's ember gems secreted aboard the *Zenobia*.

There was no doubt that Nahla was extremely smart. The level of language she was using to rewrite the old mage texts in Universal Speech far exceeded her years. Listening to her read her words out loud, it was hard to believe she was only nine years old. Perhaps that was what had made their Dark Mage brother, Castiel, want to control and torture her so much. Maybe he'd been as jealous of his sister's intelligence as he'd been of his other siblings' mage abilities.

Jace and Nahla continued to discuss mage history, with Oriana and Darius chipping in, but Carina could only listen with half an ear. Her own interface was occupying her attention as she tried to uncover some information that was proving surprisingly difficult to find.

Taking a break from her search, she let the screen fall into her lap. The information she wanted wasn't very important. All that really mattered was that the *Bathsheba* was finally free of Regians and under the Black Dogs' and her own command.

Retaking the ship had been surprisingly easy. The aliens had made the mistake of leaving only a few guards behind after they'd transferred all the human prisoners to their planet. As a result, they'd lost their strongest military advantage: huge numbers.

Once the Black Dogs and Mezban's soldiers had broken through the weak Regian defense and reached the ship's armories, the battle was quickly over. The men and women were not the undernourished, untrained, and unarmed inhabitants of poor settlements on backwater planets the aliens were accustomed to preying upon. Nor were they fresh out of stasis, unsteady and disoriented.

The troops had dispatched most of the insectoid aliens efficiently, and as soon as the mages could reach their supply of elixir, they'd finished off the remainder with Split Casts before Healing the soldiers' wounds.

No other Regian ships were approaching, and now all they had to do was to set a course for Earth and continue on their way. They could work out the finer details of the voyage later.

Carina wondered if the living starship who had brought them here had finally flown away. The Enthrall Cast should have worn off hours ago, but the last time she'd inquired, the space-faring animal had remained hanging around the *Bathsheba*. She guessed the creature would leave eventually, probably to return to the Regian planet or, if she feared recapture, perhaps she would undertake the kind of long journey the aliens used her for when they raided impoverished worlds for human hosts.

Banishing her time-wasting musings from her mind, Carina lifted the interface and opened the screen again. They had to get underway soon. The Regians might decide to mount another attack.

The problem was, in order to plot a course, they had to know their current position, but the vast spacetime anomaly drifting within and beyond the Regian system was chaotically distorting the light that passed through it. The *Bathsheba's* scanners were reporting fluctuating, unreliable data from the direction of the cloud, and, even worse, the ship's computer didn't recognize the star systems that were not obscured.

She'd been trying to get around the difficulty by using information from the navigation logs. If she knew the route the *Bathsheba* had followed since being taken off her original course, she could extrapolate their current coordinates. But the logs were incomplete, possibly due to something the Regians had done or failed to do when they took over the ship.

The door opened and Bryce walked in. The general conversation paused, and he announced, "Pappu's in the brig, and I took Calvaley straight to the sick bay after releasing him from stasis." He dropped onto the sofa next to Carina and added, as the discussion in the room resumed, "Poor guy's in a bad way."

She would never have described Calvaley as a 'poor guy', but she wasn't surprised he was suffering ill effects from his time in Deep Sleep. She'd felt terrible for days after awakening from stasis, and Calvaley was an old man.

"How bad?" she asked. "Is he going to be okay?"

"I don't know. The medics wouldn't tell me anything. They told me to get the hell out of their way or I'd end up in the sick bay too."

Carina smiled. Black Dog medics didn't mince their words. Bryce had probably gotten the polite version of what they would have said to a fellow soldier.

But then she grew serious again. Calvaley must have done terrible things in his career, though he'd excused his actions, saying they were necessary to create a unified, civilized society. His motivations had been deluded, but honorable in his own eyes, and he'd suffered plenty at the hands of Sable Dirksen, coming close to death from starvation.

If he died soon after reviving from stasis, she might feel a twinge of pity for him.

It had been that modicum of sympathy that had prompted her to take him from Deep Sleep as soon as they'd secured the ship. The longer he stayed under, the greater the threat to his life, and she had a feeling they'd all been in stasis longer than the few years originally planned upon.

"How's the course setting going?" Bryce asked.

"Not good. In fact," Carina said, putting down the screen, "if Hsiao hasn't come up with anything, I'm going to suggest we give up and just pick somewhere—anywhere—away from that screwy cloud of nonsense that's messing with the data. Then we might get our bearings and be able to set a course."

"Makes sense to me," said Bryce. "Though..." a wrinkle

formed between his brows "...do you know how much fuel we have?"

"Er, no." She'd been concentrating so hard on navigation, she hadn't even thought to check the fuel.

"My guess is, we might be low. We're way off route, right? The Regians could have used up most of it to bring us here."

"I hate to admit it, but that wouldn't surprise me," said Carina. "They probably didn't even understand the *Bathsheba's* engines or how to use the fuel efficiently. They usually travel through deep space inside living creatures, after all."

But speculating about the aliens' intellectual capacity wasn't going to get her, her family, or anyone else aboard any closer to Earth. She lifted the interface again. "So, we need a settled system where we can refuel." Though they had no idea where they were, signs of planets inhabited by humans would show on the scan data.

"Uh huh," Bryce said, scooting closer and peering at the screen. "You should probably talk to Hsiao about it."

"Yeah, you're right." But Carina had felt the events of the last few days catching up with her. She relaxed into the sofa and rested her head on its back. "In a minute."

She held Bryce's gaze for long seconds, and he held hers. She'd missed being around him, and she didn't want to be separated from him ever again.

"Hey," he said, smiling.

"Hey." She brushed his hair away from his eyes.

At the same time, Ferne groaned. "I hope you two aren't going to start *kissing!*"

"Oh, grow up and leave them alone," said Oriana.

Suddenly, Carina realized something. She sat upright. "Earlier on, I tried to figure out how long we were in stasis, but I was looking at the *Bathsheba's* old chrono, which we never really understood. I just remembered Cadwallader had one installed that marked Standard Time."

She swiped then tapped her screen.

When she read the star date that came up, she dropped it in her lap.

"What's wrong?" asked Bryce.

She turned to him and stared into his eyes. "We've been underway for *seventy-three years*."

He whistled. "No wonder Calvaley looked so bad." However, after considering for a moment, he went on, "But it's not that important, is it? We all survived stasis, we're just a little bit older."

"Seventy-three years on a colony ship? Do you have any idea how far we must have traveled? How much farther we must be from Earth than we were before?"

"Well, it has to be as a seventy-three-year journey, plus the distance we still had to travel on our original course, I guess. Maybe we can cut across?"

Carina rolled her eyes. "How can you think this is no big deal?"

Bryce's happy, teasing look suddenly faded, and he paused, troubled.

She took his hand.

The duration of their journey plus the effects of time dilation would mean Bryce's parents were already long dead, and it was likely the same was true of his brothers and sisters. Such was the great tragedy of long-distance space travel. Embarking on an inter-sector voyage usually meant saying goodbye to loved ones forever.

"You're thinking about your family, right?" She'd never met the people who had abandoned him while he was suffering from Ithiyan plague, later returning and paying for his treatment. Now, she never would.

He heaved a deep sigh. "It's okay. I knew when I decided to come with you I'd probably never see them again."

But the Regians' hijack of the *Bathsheba* had turned that 'probably' into 'definitely'.

She squeezed his hand tighter, and he managed a strained smile.

"The way I see it," he said, "the longer our trip takes the more time I get to spend hanging out with you. Also, who knows what's going to happen? When we finally reach Earth we might regret it and decide to go back, so we'll be cooped up together even longer."

"Hmm. I like your first thought better."

"So do I."

Carina's comm announced a request from Hsiao.

"What's up?" she asked the pilot, hoping for good news.

"Have you seen the latest scanner data?" Hsiao asked. "That time-shifting nebulosity is on the move, and it's heading our way."

arina approached the *Bathsheba's* bridge, on her way to discuss the approaching cloud of anomalous spacetime with Hsiao. It was a place she'd rarely been during her time on the ship. In the months before she'd entered Deep Sleep, she'd preferred to leave the day-to-day running of the ship to Cadwallader.

Passing through the entrance doors triggered detailed memories of the lieutenant colonel, and a wave of grief washed over her. She'd gotten so used to the man's presence in her life, it was hard to believe she would never set eyes on him again.

In her early days as a merc, Cadwallader had been an object of fear to her. The man had been such a hard-ass, merciless taskmaster, one stern look from him was all that was required to instantly bring every soldier in the vicinity into line. But since she and the Black Dogs had become reacquainted, she'd glimpsed another side to him. She'd come to understand his love for the long-dead John Speidel, and, occasionally, gentleness and concern for her had broken through his adamantine facade.

She wished she'd gotten to know more of that side of him

before he died. The requirements to maintain and control of a bunch of aggressive misfits must have made his life a lonely one.

"I don't think we're in any trouble *just* yet," said Hsiao, apparently reacting to Carina's facial expression.

"I was thinking about something else," she replied, sitting down at the navigator's station. "Can you bring up a holo of what we're facing?"

Hsiao spoke to the interface on her seat arm, the lights dimmed, and a holo appeared in the center of the bridge.

Carina recognized the Regians' star system: four gas giants and the creatures' own rocky planet in orbit around an M-type star. The cloud she'd first seen while aboard the *Duchess*, fleeing the Regians, floated within the system and extended deep into space. The *Bathsheba's* computer represented the anomaly as a slowly shifting amorphous gray mass, through which the light of the Regian system's star and planets shone fitfully.

As she watched, she could see the movement Hsiao had reported. A finger was reaching out, slow and lazy, though in fact it must have been moving extremely fast. She guessed that the same sort of event had probably caused the deaths of Lomang, Mezban, and several soldiers.

She said to Hsiao, "People died when that thing edged into our flight path, but I think that was because they were inside a moving ship. The cloud jumped them forward or backward in time a little bit, and when they re-entered normal time, the ship had moved away."

Hsiao shrugged.

Carina continued, "What's going to happen if the cloud hits us while the *Bathsheba's* stationary? Maybe nothing at all."

"Your guess is as good as mine," said the pilot. "Is there any point in speculating? We should get out of the damned thing's way. I would have moved the *Bathsheba* as soon as I saw the cloud approaching, except we aren't in immediate danger and I didn't like to do anything absent a direct order. Who's in command now that Cadwallader and Atoi have passed? You?"

Carina grimaced at the proposal. She wasn't sure she wanted to be responsible for everyone aboard. Responsibility for her family was enough for her for the time being. "I hadn't thought about it. We're all still settling down after our escape. But, about the anomaly, have you tried to find out our position?"

Hsiao also grimaced, in reply.

"Exactly," said Carina. "This isn't Geriel Sector. It isn't any sector on the *Bathsheba's* data base. We're in uncharted space, right? How many more of these spacetime anomalies might be out there? What happens if we crash through another one while underway and all of us blink out of time synchronicity?"

The pilot shook her head. "I'm not sure your guess about what happened to Lomang and the others is correct. If the cloud timeshifted the people we lost, why didn't it timeshift part of the creature we were flying inside, too? You can't argue that it only affects living creatures because the ship was alive."

"I thought about that. The starship comes from the same planet as the Regians, so it must have evolved their ability to move in time, too."

"And it understood *we* couldn't do that so it decided to help us out by evading the cloud?" Hsiao asked skeptically.

"It isn't impossible," replied Carina. "Do you have a different explanation?"

"No, but that doesn't make yours correct. Anyway, this is all moot. If the *Bathsheba* stops too fast while traveling at even low speed we'll all be messy puddles. Trying to slow to a full stop wouldn't be wise if we do encounter another cloud. The best thing we can do if we encounter one is to alter our trajectory to go around it, if it's possible to do it in time."

"But you're the only one who can fly the ship. I mean, I could try, but..."

Hsiao moved both of her hands over the flight controls protectively.

Carina lifted her lip at one corner. "Very funny. My point is, unless you plan on spending the rest of your natural days and then some flying the *Bathsheba*, you'll have to go into stasis. And while you're out of commission, who's going to alter our flight path?"

"Some of the mercs have flying basics under their belts, you included."

"But do you think I could navigate around a cloud like that without putting us all in jeopardy?"

"You're right," said Hsiao. "Depending on how far away we are when we spot a cloud, if we're traveling at top speed, you might not have time to alter course to avoid it. I might find it hard myself."

"And we *must* travel at top speed," Carina said.

"But maybe you're being too pessimistic," the pilot went on. "Who's to say we're going to meet another one of those things? Let's just deal with this one. Then we can worry about any others lying in wait."

While they'd been talking the finger sprouting from the anomaly groped closer, a great puff of aberrant physical law pushing in their direction.

"It's going to reach us in a few hours," said Hsiao.

"Okay," Carina said. "Do you want to do the honors?"

"Sure." Hsiao focused on the flight controls. "Any particular direction you favor?"

"Away from here."

"That's nice and easy." The pilot opened her controls and studied the screen. Then suddenly she bent closer toward it, as if she couldn't believe what she was seeing. "*Son of a bitch!*"

"What's wrong?"

Hsiao turned to Carina, her eyes wide and disbelieving. "We're out of fuel. We've got nothing, not a gram. We're dead in space."

Carina got up and strode to the pilot's station. "How come?" She could understand it if they were *low* on fuel. The Regians had flown the colony ship awfully far. But it was too much of a coincidence that the ship had entirely run out at exactly the moment the aliens had arrived at their system. "Are you looking at the right gauge?"

"Of *course* I am," Hsiao replied irritably.

"Then, I don't get it." Carina checked the readings herself, but the pilot was correct. Unless there was a gremlin in the *Bathsheba's* system, the ship's tanks were empty.

"I think I might," said Hsiao. She brought up a different screen, displaying short-range scanner data.

"Bastards," Carina murmured.

The scanners were picking up a large mass of deuterium-tritium. It could mean only one thing: at some point during the battle for the ship, the Regians had emptied the fuel tanks.

They'd understood more about starships than she'd given them credit for. Realizing they couldn't win, the aliens had decided to strand their vanquishers.

"Maybe we aren't totally screwed," said Hsiao. "We still have the *Peregrine*. If the Regians didn't also dump her fuel she could tow the *Bathsheba*. It'll be slow going, but it's better than nothing."

"*If* they didn't dump her fuel too," Carina said. "Actually, that isn't the biggest concern right now. What else is going on out there? Anything new happening on the Regian planet?"

Hsiao switched screens again. "Yeahhh...there is something. Wait a minute. I'll feed this through to the holo."

Carina straightened up to look at the 3D image of the planet.

At first, the surface only appeared marked by tiny specks.

Like the light from the world, the specks flickered, shifting marginally in time due to the effect of the gray cloud.

"Uh oh," said Hsiao. "I don't like the look of them."

Neither did Carina.

The specks grew larger, taking on a distinct shape: the gentle sloping dome of the living starships the Regians had enslaved.

It could mean only one thing: the aliens had evacuated the *Bathsheba's* fuel tanks not out of pure spite but in order to give themselves time to launch a second attack on the ship.

"Shit," said Hsiao. "What are we going to do?"

"Check the *Peregrine's* tanks."

"On it," the pilot replied, rising from her seat.

"You can't do it from here?"

"Nope. The techs could never marry the two systems. I'll comm you when I know."

As Hsiao left, Carina returned her attention to the holo. The creatures the Regians flew had grown a little larger, but it would still take them hours to reach the *Bathsheba*—enough time to evacuate everyone to the *Peregrine* and leave, if necessary.

However, she suspected Hsiao would discover the Regians weren't so dumb as to leave the humans a ship to get away in. Also, the *Bathsheba* was essential to her plan to reach Earth. Without the colony ship, they would never do it. The best they could hope if they left on the *Peregrine* was to discover a habitable planet where no one wanted to kill them.

They should stand their ground and fight, but there were a hell of a lot of Regians on their way, and the aliens had defeated them before through sheer force of numbers.

Suddenly, Carina found herself missing Cadwallader more than ever.

What would the lieutenant colonel have done?

3

P arthenia watched Carina suiting up, her expression sad but resolute. Parthenia's feelings were the same. Just when they could finally resume their long voyage to Earth, yet another obstacle stood in their way, and this one seemed insurmountable. The Regians had stranded them, emptying even the *Peregrine's* fuel tanks, and now the aliens were about to attack.

The injustice of it all made her bitter. They'd fought so hard and been through so much, why couldn't they get just one break? One thing that would come easy to them, that they didn't have to fight tooth and nail for?

She snapped her helmet locks in place and gently sucked on the tube that connected to her elixir reservoir. A small amount of the sour liquid spurted into her mouth.

As she looked up again, she saw Carina crossing the armory, walking toward her.

Her sister's face was grave as she put a hand on Parthenia's shoulder. "I just want to be sure you understand. You have to protect the kids first, the same as last time, okay? I'm relying on you."

"Is it going to be the same as before, though?" Parthenia asked.

The previous battle with the Regians had been short and decisive. The mages hadn't needed to Cast Split much—they'd focused on Healing the soldiers who had been burned with acid during the initial assault.

From the demeanor of her sister and the men and women around her, no one expected things to go so smoothly this time around.

"Honestly? I don't know," Carina replied. "We don't know exactly how many Regians are coming, but if those ships are only carrying a few hundred of them each, we're going to have a hard time. We have to prevent them from boarding, then we should be okay. But if they break through somehow, we're gonna be swamped. I don't know if it's much consolation, but if that happens and we lose, the Regians might decide not to use mages as hosts."

Revulsion swept over Parthenia as she recalled the time she'd spent as the aliens' captive—the dreadful cold, darkness, and humidity of their planet; her desperate attempts to make elixir to save her brothers and sisters; and how she'd forced her way through suffocating soil to make her escape. "I'm not going back to that place. I swear, I'd rather die."

Carina looked down for a moment as if debating how to respond. When she raised her face, it was full of fire. "That's the *wrong* attitude! You have to survive, Parthenia, no matter what. You must *live*. You never know what might happen. I don't want you to ever give up, okay? Even if the situation seems hopeless. Promise me you won't give up."

Parthenia chewed her lip.

Carina grabbed both her shoulders and gave her a gentle shake. "Promise me!"

"Okay! I promise."

"Good. I have to go now. When the battle begins, stay at the back with Darius and Nahla, at a safe distance. Cast Split to help us out when you can, of course, but your priority is the youngsters. Jace won't be there to help you. He's at another airlock with Ferne and Oriana. I need you to do this for me."

"All right. I hear you."

Carina nodded, appearing satisfied, and then returned to the group of soldiers who were still suiting up.

Her sister had taken command, as she had in the earlier battle. She seemed the obvious candidate, given her military experience and her knowledge of what the mages could do, and no one had objected.

Parthenia understood why Carina had made her responsible for the protection of their siblings: she couldn't organize the defense of the ship *and* safeguard their brothers and sisters. Her sister's instruction didn't feel like an imposition, as once it would have. Parthenia wasn't sure why—if Carina had changed or she had.

A hand touched her arm.

She turned to see Kamil.

"I wanted to—" he said, but before he could finish, Parthenia hugged him tight, their armored chests crushing together.

After a moment of surprise, he hugged her back.

"I was going to come and find you," said Parthenia, "after we messaged. But I had to make sure my brothers and sisters were settled in."

"It's okay," he replied. "I also thought we'd have plenty of time to see each other. I didn't want to crowd you. You've been through a lot."

"We all have. Oh, I wish you had come to see me, or I'd gone to see you."

"It can't be helped now. We weren't to know what would happen."

They'd been holding each other awkwardly as they talked.

Parthenia let go of Kamil and looked up at his face, visible through his open visor.

She wanted to kiss him. It might be her last opportunity. But she couldn't do it unless they took off their helmets, and it was too late for that.

"When this is over, we shouldn't wait to meet up," she said.

"No, we shouldn't," Kamil agreed. "Not this time. As soon as the battle's finished, I'll comm you."

"Or I'll comm you. As soon as it's over."

Kamil gave her a long look without speaking, and Parthenia understood his unspoken meaning. They were both thinking the same thing: their chances of seeing each other again were slim.

A lump swelled in her throat. Life was so unfair. Why couldn't they have had more time together? Her chin trembled, and Kamil's face blurred in her vision.

"Just try not to get hurt, okay?" she mumbled.

Through her tears, she saw him smile. "Not getting hurt is my number one tactic."

Parthenia swallowed. "How can you joke about it?"

In a more serious tone, Kamil answered, "It's the only way to get through it."

Then his features brightened once more. "Anyway, if I do get hurt, you can save me again."

"I'm not a magician! If you're seriously wounded, I can't—"

He raised a gloved hand and placed his forefinger on her lips, repeating, "I'll comm you as soon as the battle's finished."

As he went to join his group, who were heading out to guard one of the airlocks, Parthenia watched him.

Carina comm'd Bryce. She'd sent him with Ferne, Oriana, Jace, and the mercs Halliday and Jackson to the airlock that adjoined the Deep Sleep chamber. Thirty more Black Dogs accompanied them, while she'd kept most of Mezban's soldiers with her. Due to their commander's traitorous actions, she didn't fully trust them.

"All set?" she asked him.

"All set. How about you?"

"We're nearly ready. Just about to head out."

"Got an ETA on the Regians?"

"Hsiao reckons another six minutes until the ships arrive."

"It's a pity we can't blast them before they get here."

The soldiers in the armory were ready and awaiting orders. Carina told them to follow her. She was going to lead the defense of the main airlock.

As she strode from the chamber she continued her conversation with Bryce. "Yeah, but we can't fire a shot without any juice."

Without fuel, the *Bathsheba's* space armaments were useless. Her human passengers were her only defense.

They had to prevent the hordes of aliens from gaining a foothold inside the ship. If the Regians broke through the line of resistance at any of the airlocks, it would all be over. Like a rising tide, the aliens would sweep in, overwhelming anyone who stood in their way.

"At least a tough decision's been taken out of our hands," said Bryce. "It wouldn't feel right to hurt the living starships."

The objection had occurred to Carina, too, before she realized the *Bathsheba's* weapons were dead anyway. The creatures were acting against their will in bringing the aliens to mount a second assault. Hurting them would have felt very wrong

"Yeah, I guess in a way we're lucky it's out of our hands," she said.

"How many ships are coming?"

"Fifty-eight."

"*Fifty-eight?*"

Carina didn't answer. There was nothing she could say to make their situation seem better.

"And how many Regians is that?" Bryce asked.

"You saw how big the ship that brought us here was. She could accommodate two or three hundred human beings. As to how many Regians would fit aboard one of them, it has to be the same amount, maybe more if they squeeze them in."

Bryce seemed lost for words.

"When they arrive we'll have a better idea about where they're going to concentrate their forces," said Carina. "I may move some troops and mages around according to where the fighting is heaviest."

"We'll be listening for orders."

"I know. Good luck."

"You, too," Bryce replied. He didn't close the comm, however, and neither could Carina bring herself to do it. Silence hung between them like a suffocating blanket.

She'd arrived at the main airlock. She checked the time. The Regians were due in three minutes, yet she still couldn't say anything more to Bryce or close the channel linking them.

He was the first to crack. "Carina, I—"

"Don't say it."

She heard his breathy sigh.

"We might not see each other again," he said.

"It's a strong possibility, I admit, but, please, let's not go there, huh? I just can't. It's too much."

"If you say so." Bryce's tone was pained.

She was also hurting, but the idea of speaking as if they would never see each other again only hurt worse.

"I'll keep you updated," she said crisply, and closed the comm at last.

4

Ranks of mercs faced the main portal into the *Bathsheba*. Carina had Locked the airlock hatch, and it was her fervent hope that the simple Cast would be all it took to deter the Regians from furthering their attack. If only the aliens would burn themselves out on repeated attempts to force the hatch mechanism to open, and simply give up and go home.

It was an unlikely outcome.

The mechanism itself was weak. The Regians had repaired the acid damage from their initial attack, but the repairs had been poorly done—the aliens were not used to working with inanimate starships. It wouldn't take much to breach the seals again, so a lot hung on the mages' Locks. But if the aliens melted them away entirely, there would be nothing there to Lock, and the Casts would fail.

Also, though the mages could Cast for a long time, they couldn't do so indefinitely. Exhaustion would overcome them eventually, and then, when the Regians poured through, they would have no energy left to Split them or Heal wounded soldiers. Deciding exactly when to give up Casting Lock in order to conserve energy would be a hard call to make.

The Regians might also try to enter the ship via other routes. The *Bathsheba* had the usual additional exit—and entry —points: garbage chutes. If they had no luck at the airlocks, the aliens might try to get in via one or more chutes. Carina had stationed a handful of mercs at each one, making entering the ship that way a suicide mission, but that was no deterrent to the Regians.

And then there was the roof to the twilight dome. The Regians had done a similarly bad job there as they had with the airlock mechanisms. The roof was airtight, but it wasn't strong, and if the aliens possessed anything like the explosive she'd used to blow it open, they could easily arrive at the same result. She hadn't stationed many defenders in that part of the ship, bargaining on her impression that the Regians weren't sufficiently technologically advanced to make bombs.

"One minute," said Hsiao over Carina's comm.

She looked over her shoulder to where Darius, Nahla, and Parthenia crouched in a doorway, way back from the engagement zone yet within sight of it. She'd made the difficult decision to bring Nahla along even though the little girl couldn't do much to help. She'd told her that if the aliens broke in she was to move out of sight of the battle, but she hadn't wanted to leave her alone in a room somewhere or devote soldiers for her defense. It would only be delaying the inevitable.

The minute had to be nearly up. Carina tensed, waiting for the bump. One or more of the living starships would have to collide with the stationary *Bathsheba* for the aliens to attempt to board.

As her thought completed, the softest of impacts shifted the floor under her feet. Another two or three bumps followed the first in quick succession.

"This is it," Carina said over a general comm. "Mages and mercs, prepare for attack."

A subtle ripple passed through the soldiers as they tightened their hold on their weapons, altered position slightly, or only stiffened.

She fixed her gaze on the portal, while also registering the chrono on her HUD. The Lock Cast would last another five to eight minutes. Before five minutes was up she would Cast again.

Go home. Go away, and find some other hosts elsewhere. Or stick to your own cold, wet, soulless planet and die out.

"Where are the starships?" she asked the pilot. "Are they at both airlocks?"

"They're everywhere," came the reply.

"Everywhere? All over the ship?"

That didn't make any sense. The Regians should have been clustering at one airlock at least.

"Well, not exactly *all* over the ship," Hsiao went on. "As they got near to us they spread out, and now they're distributing themselves along the starboard side. Can't you feel them hitting us?"

Now that the pilot mentioned it, Carina realized she'd continued to feel minute impacts against the ship.

"Right. So...how many are near the Deep Sleep chamber airlock?"

"None of them are near that."

"Are you sure?"

"I think I know how to read close-range scanner data, Lin," the pilot replied tersely.

"But I don't see why they..." Carina's words petered out as she tried to figure out what the Regians were up to.

"Your guess is as good as mine."

A minute or so stretched out in suspenseful silence. Carina felt no further impacts.

"What's happening now?" she asked Hsiao.

"More of the same. They've all reached us, and they're pressed up against the starboard bulkhead."

"What the—"

"And get this," the pilot continued, "the friendly one that brought us here has joined them."

For a few seconds, Carina was speechless. Eventually, she said, "So, she's decided to side with the Regians? After all they did to her?"

Before Hsiao could answer, a comm request arrived from Bryce.

"Excuse me a moment," Carina said. Then, to Bryce, "If you were going to ask me what's happening, I don't have a clue."

She explained what the pilot had told her so far.

"I think I can take a guess on what's happening," said Bryce.

"You can?"

"The Regians plan on boring us to death."

Carina rolled her eyes.

"Did you just roll your eyes?" he asked.

"Quit kidding about. This is serious. I can't organize an effective defense if I don't have any idea how we might be attacked."

"Sorry. The only thing I can suggest is they're waiting for something."

"Yeah, you could be right. Maybe they're waiting for rein-forcements. It's the only explanation that makes any sense."

Great, she thought. *Just great.* They would be hard pressed to deter the numbers of Regians who had already arrived, let alone even more of them.

"I'd better talk to the other teams," she told Bryce.

She sent a comm to the team leaders, explaining the situation and telling them to keep everyone on standby until further notice. Then she spoke to Hsiao, asking if there had been any changes.

"Negative. The starwhales haven't moved."

"Starwhales?"

"We have to give them a name. It kinda fits, don't you think?"

"Yeah, whatever. I just wish they would *do* something."

"The suspense is killing me, too."

"Wait. I have an idea," said Carina. "Maybe the Regians are using their acid to try to burn through the hull, avoiding the airlocks altogether."

"Hmm," Hsiao said. "Give me a second." After a pause, she added, "Nope. Sensors are saying everything's fine and dandy with the hull."

"*Shit.* What the hell's going on?"

Time dragged by without any movement from the Regians or the starwhales. Carina's muscles ached with the tension of waiting to be attacked, and she grew more confused and apprehensive.

No more starwhales arrived from the Regian planet. The animals remained in their positions pressed up against the Bathsheba, though Hsiao reported that occasionally one would leave, fly around for a short while, and then return to its spot, as if stretching its wings or going on a short trip just for something to do.

The mercs were starting to fidget, and more than a few had allowed their pulse rifles to droop.

Finally, Carina felt compelled to issue a wide *At ease* command. The soldiers under her immediate control relaxed.

But as one of Mezban's men lowered his weapon, the muzzle brushed the leg of one of the Black Dogs. The woman objected, violently pushing him and causing him to stumble into another soldier. The man righted himself and immediately pushed her back.

The Black Dog's visor snapped open, and she yelled a string

of expletives at him. Other Black Dogs began to square up against the new soldiers, who turned to face them.

"Cut it out!" yelled Carina. "Resume your positions!"

The mercs instantly obeyed. The offended woman's visor lowered and she lifted her rifle. Mezban's men were slower to react, but two or three beats later they were also in defense-ready mode.

The wait went on.

5

In the end, Carina was forced to tell everyone to stand down. After an hour and a half of maintaining their positions, ready to defend the ship, nothing at all had happened. The Regians remained outside in their starwhales, glued to the ship, but not making a single move to attack.

She told Hsiao to let her know immediately there was any change in the positions of the living starships or signs that the Regians were emerging from them. the soldiers to remain on alert, suited up and with their weapons within reach, but otherwise to resume their regular duties.

She began to walk back to the bridge to talk to Hsiao, comm'ing Bryce to meet her there.

It seemed bizarre to return to normality while thousands of time-shifting aliens were hanging around outside the ship, ready to seize the humans and turn them into living hosts to their offspring, but what other choice was there? Opening the airlocks and going out to fight the Regians aboard their starwhales would be madness. The enemy vastly outnumbered the soldiers, and opening the airlocks would make the *Bathsheba* vulnerable.

Perhaps that was what the Regians were waiting for? Were the aliens besieging them, knowing that eventually they would run out of food and then they would be forced to take desperate measures?

If so, the Regians were in for a long wait. The *Bathsheba's* stores would last for years, and when they were finally gone, they could program the waste recycling facilities to produce nutritional bars. No one would like to eat them, knowing what they were made from, but it would be better than starving.

Or maybe the attackers were hoping that, without fuel, the colony ship would become too cold to sustain human life. Carina guessed it would in the end, but they had emergency power, the *Bathsheba* was huge, and the vacuum of space was a wonderful insulator. They would be more likely to starve to death before they froze.

The bridge door opened before her, and Hsiao spun around in her pilot's seat as Carina went inside.

She threw herself into the captain's seat and took off her helmet.

The petite pilot seemed mildly amused. "Who'd have thought, huh?"

"I wish I knew what they're planning."

"Do you want to see them?"

"Sure."

A moment later a holo of the *Bathsheba* appeared in the center of the bridge. The starwhales protruded from one side of the ship, looking like parasites sucking the blood from a big, ugly fish.

Carina wrinkled her nose. "What I can't figure out is, why did the one we rescued join them? Why didn't she get away while she could? When they get the chance, the Regians will board her and tie that thing to her insides again."

"I don't think they have yet," said Hsiao. "The scanners haven't picked up anything emerging from the ships."

Carina could only shake her head in bewilderment.

"So, now we just wait?" asked the pilot.

"What choice do we have? We can't go anywhere."

The bridge door opened and Bryce came in. He strode to the captain's seat, swooped down, and quickly kissed Carina on the lips.

"You're on duty," she admonished, though not strongly.

"I'm going to take all the chances I get," he replied. "We might all die soon,"

Hsiao had swung her seat around to face away from them.

"You don't have to be so cheerful about it," said Carina.

"We might have more hours, days, or even months. What's not to be cheerful about?"

"I suppose you could look at it like that. To me it feels more like standing in front of a firing squad, waiting for them to shoot."

"We've escaped from worse situations," said Bryce.

"We have?"

Carina was considering the truth of what he was saying, weighing up the dangers they'd faced against being stranded without fuel with thousands of hostile aliens at the door, when Darius Sent to her.

"Can I talk to you?" he asked. "Or are you busy?"

She mentally replied, "You know you don't have to Send, right? You can comm me."

"Oh, yeah." His soft giggle echoed in her mind. "I forgot."

She held up a hand to Bryce, who'd been about to say something, and said to Darius, "What do you want to tell me?"

"I don't think we're in any danger," he replied.

Carina learned long ago to always listen to her Spirit Mage brother, even when he didn't seem to be making any sense.

"What makes you think we aren't in danger, sweetheart?"

"The starship animals are happy. I can feel their emotions, like really strong hot chocolate."

"Their happiness feels like hot chocolate?" she asked, drawing a look of surprise from Bryce, who could only hear her half of the conversation. Hsiao also peered over her shoulder, giving Carina a quizzical look.

"That's the best way I can describe it," Darius said.

"They aren't in pain, like the one we flew in was at first?" She'd been worried her youngest brother would be sensing the agony of all the starwhales. It had nearly crippled him before.

"No," he replied, "they're really happy. And I figured, if they're happy, then the Regians can't be controlling them."

"You think they aren't being controlled?" Carina repeated in a daze, her confusion only increasing. Could it be possible the Regians weren't piloting the starwhales? And if so, why had the creatures flown to the *Bathsheba*?

"Thanks for letting me know, Darius," she said. "That's really helpful," she added before closing the comm, though she wasn't clear yet on exactly what her brother's revelation meant.

After she related to Bryce and Hsiao what Darius had said, an idea occurred to her. "Do you think it's possible the starwhales aren't even carrying Regians? That they're empty...and wild, maybe?"

"That would explain the missing attack," said Bryce, "but, if you're right, why did the starwhales come here?"

"On my home planet," Hsiao said, "some birds fly in huge flocks, and when they aren't flying around they perch on trees in huge crowds, sometimes breaking branches with their weight. Maybe the starwhales have come here to join the one we freed, and now they're just...er...hanging out?"

Carina slowly nodded. "We're all suited up and armed, ready to defend the ship from a bunch of space-faring animals who just wanted to *hang out*."

"You know," Bryce said, "I prefer that scenario to what we thought was happening."

"Me, too," said Carina. "It's way better than the alternative.

But, if we're right, has anything really changed? We're stuck here with no way of leaving. The Regians can still come and attack us."

"But we have a little more time to come up with a solution," Hsiao pointed out.

"I guess so," said Carina, though she doubted a solution existed. They couldn't magic fuel out of nowhere, or make the Regian threat disappear.

'Aw, shit," Hsiao said, staring at her interface.

"What's wrong?" asked Carina, imagining the pilot was about to announce their speculation had been disproved—that the starwhales were finally moving toward the airlocks, and the Regian attack was about to begin.

But the pilot didn't answer. She adjusted the controls on the holo display. The image of the *Bathsheba*, which had remained hanging in the air, disappeared and was replaced by the earlier holo of the Regian planetary system and surrounding space.

"We forgot about it," she said, "but the creepy cloud is still creeping up on us."

The long tongue of anomalous space was reaching out toward the *Bathsheba* like a frog catching a fly in slow motion.

"*Dammit,*" breathed Carina.

The threat to their safety hadn't gone away, it had only reverted to the previous one.

"How long until it reaches us?" she asked.

"Its rate of expansion isn't steady," Hsiao answered. "The computer estimates the tip will hit the ship in between forty-eight minutes and three hours fifteen."

6

"Where's Parthenia?" Carina asked as soon as she entered her family's suite. Her other siblings were all there and in the midst of their usual activities, but her oldest sister was nowhere to be seen. "Is she in the bathroom?"

"We don't know where she is," Oriana replied. "She said she was going to see a friend, but that's all she would say."

Carina wondered if the 'friend' was the boy she'd mistakenly defended Parthenia against one time. If so, she couldn't blame her sister for wanting to be with him in the current circumstances, when no one knew how long they had left.

Yet she'd hoped the family could be together while they waited out the latest crisis. The spacetime anomaly was stretching out toward them, and it seemed likely the ship would eventually be enveloped by the cloud.

What might happen then was anyone's guess. The *Bathsheba* was completely motionless, and there was no threat of her moving while affected by the anomaly—but did the cloud affect living and non-living things in the same way? And if half of the ship were covered by the cloud, would that part slip forward or backward in time, shearing away from the unaffected half?

A hull breach like that would mean near-instant death for everyone aboard.

Carina sat on the sofa next to Darius, who was lying on his front and playing a card game with Nahla, though she also had an interface open and was reading while waiting for her brother to take his turn.

"Do the starwhales still feel happy?" Carina asked Darius.

He looked upward for a moment as he found out the answer, and then nodded. "Yeah. It's a nice feeling."

She wished he could communicate with the creatures. Then she would have a much better idea of their intentions, and maybe she could ask them a huge favor. Were they really just 'hanging out'?

If only she could Send to the starwhales. When she was a little girl, she'd often tried to speak to animals by Casting Send, but always without success. Once or twice she'd also tried the Cast with humans, though without Nai Nai's knowledge—the old lady would have been furious with her for taking the risk. The result had been the same. Send only worked between mages.

On the other hand, anything was worth a try.

The only problem was, how to do it? If the object of the Cast wasn't in sight, the mage needed some kind of connection to him or her, usually a personal item of some kind. Yet they'd taken no part of the starwhale with them when they'd left her. Without something to tie them to the ship mentally, they had no way to reach it.

Except, maybe...

"Darius," she said.

Something in her tone made him put down his cards and look at her.

"Can you *feel* which is the starwhale we traveled on, separately from the others?" she asked.

"Oh, sure. I can feel her. That one's our friend. She likes me and you because we took away her pain."

"She can tell us apart from the other humans?"

"Of course," Darius replied, his look indicating Carina was being a little dumb.

His connection with the creature appeared to be stronger than a simple sensitivity to her feelings.

"So..." said Carina tentatively, "if you tried to Send to her... she might understand you?"

Darius replied, "I can try. What do you want me to say to her?"

"Could you ask her what she and her friends are doing here, and if they could help us?"

"Okay. I think I can remember that." Darius got up and padded across the room to a jug of elixir on a side cabinet. He lifted the lid and poured a small amount into a glass, and then drank it.

As he closed his eyes, an expression of concentration appeared on his young face.

"What's Darius Casting?" Oriana asked. She and Ferne had been drawing designs for clothes they wanted to print, oblivious to the conversation between Carina and her brother.

Carina hadn't yet broadcast the bad news about the approaching cloud. There didn't seemed to be any point, at least not until the approach of the anomaly was imminent, when she would have to say something to give everyone a chance to say their last goodbyes in case the worst happened.

"He's trying to Send to the creature we Enthralled to bring us here."

Oriana nodded and returned her attention to her design, but then she looked up again and said, "Why?"

"I'll tell you in a minute," Carina replied, focused on Darius, whose lips were silently moving as a crease formed between his eyebrows.

"That'll *never* work," said Ferne. "Believe me. When we were on Ithiya, I tried to Send to our pets loads of times. I thought it would be cool to talk to them. No luck."

"I'm not so sure you're right," Carina said, watching Darius.

The young boy was clearly having a conversation. Unless he was talking to himself, he could only be chatting with the starwhale.

Suddenly, his lips stopped moving and he opened his eyes. "What did you want me to ask her?"

"What?!" Carina stood up. "You could talk to her? What did she say?"

"Uh...First I said hello, just to check if she could hear me, and I found out she could! Then I told her my name, and I asked her if she was doing okay."

Ferne laughed. "Hurry up and get to the important part!"

"Let him speak," Nahla admonished.

"She said she was okay," said Darius, unfazed by Ferne's urging, "and she asked me how I was doing. I said I was fine and I thanked her kindly for bringing us to our ship."

Ferne let out a heavy sigh.

"And *she* said," Darius went on, "she would have brought us here anyway, even if we hadn't made her do it."

Ooops, Carina thought, feeling bad for Enthralling the creature. "I hope you apologized for what we did."

"Of course," Darius said. "It's cool to talk to her. Her voice sounds raspy and deep, like a big frog. I don't hear any words, but somehow I understand what she's saying."

"And then did you ask her what she and her friends are doing, and if they might help us?"

"No. I forgot that part."

"Oh my goodness!" Carina exclaimed. "Send to her again. Hurry up."

While Darius was sipping Elixir to continue his chat with the starwhale, she comm'd Hsiao. "Any news on the cloud?"

"Yeah, but it isn't good. It's speeding up. It's like it wants to grab us."

"What's its ETA now?"

"At the current rate of acceleration..." Hsiao paused "...eight minutes fifty-two seconds to contact with the starboard bow."

The starwhales were clustered to starboard. Hope sparked in Carina's chest, but she kept it to herself, not knowing if she was being too optimistic.

"Should I tell everyone?" Hsiao asked.

"Not yet," she replied, adding as an explanation for her reluctance, "We don't even know if it's going to hurt us."

"I was thinking," said Hsiao, "if the Regians evolved to time-shift due to the regular encroachment of the cloud, it must exert a selective pressure on them. I haven't figured it out yet, but I believe it has something to do with the planet's rotation. If they were moved out of the regular progression of time, would they remain in synch with the planet's surface? Wouldn't the planet also be time-shifted, but perhaps not in the same way?"

"Who knows?" Then Carina found she couldn't contain her excitement any longer. "We might have a solution to our problem. Standby." As she closed the comm, she turned to Darius, who had finished his second conversation and was waiting to report to her.

"She said, would we like her and her friends to push us away from the space bubble? I tried to ask her about the other stuff but she said there isn't a lot of time."

"Yes," Carina replied urgently. "Tell her yes, could she please help us?"

With a look of quiet stoicism, Darius took a third drink of elixir.

"What space bubble?" asked Oriana.

Carina replied, "You know the thing that affected Lomang,

Mezban, and the soldiers, when we were escaping from the Regian planet?"

Oriana's eyes grew wide. "That's coming near us?! Why didn't you say anything?"

"I was kind of distracted by the impending Regian attack! And then, well..."

"What could you have done about it even if you knew?" Ferne asked his twin.

"If I'm about to vanish, I want to be told about it!"

As far as Carina understood, Lomang, Mezban, and the others hadn't actually *vanished*, they'd suffocated in space while their blood boiled in their veins and air exploded from their lungs. But she judged it wasn't the right time to correct her sister.

Suddenly, the ship jerked, and then slowly they began to move.

"It worked!" Nahla shouted. "We're moving!" She jumped down from the sofa and ran to Darius to give him a hug. "You're so clever."

He smiled shyly and flushed pink.

"You saved us, Darius," Carina said. "What would we do without you?"

7

Where they were going, Carina didn't know. The most important thing was they were moving away from the spacetime anomaly, pushed by the starwhales. When they were far beyond it, the *Bathsheba's* computer might be able to recognize surrounding star patterns and tell them where they were. They might also find an inhabited planet where they could stop and refuel. The starwhales hadn't said how long they were prepared to help the humans, but they couldn't rely on the creatures' benevolence forever.

When they'd refueled, they would plot a course for Earth.

She was standing in the twilight dome, looking up at the stars. The starwhales weren't visible from her vantage point, but she could imagine the huge, silent creatures flying them onward, ripples pulsating through the thick frills that ran along their sides.

She'd come to the dome to see how the repairs were coming along. No one had managed to fabricate the transparent material of the original covering, and so men and women in EVA suits outside the ship were replacing the areas blown out by Mezban's bomb with sections of regular hull.

The remaining, unharmed area of 'window' area could be replaced with hull material, too. Its weakness was a liability. If the ship were attacked again, that would be the first place to be targeted. Carina had debated with herself long and hard about blocking up the transparent ceiling.

In the end, she'd put the question to a vote, and the majority had voted to retain it. Without even asking around, she knew why: years of space travel inside glorified tin cans resulted in a hunger for wide vistas and open skies. The ability to look out upon a starscape—no matter how cold and hard the view—wasn't something many were prepared to give up in a hurry, despite the risk.

And with the many, many years of journeying they had ahead of them, the few small pleasures they had available would make a big difference.

"I thought I might find you here," said a familiar voice behind her.

Carina smiled and turned to see Bryce.

"I was just checking to see how things are going," she said. "They've nearly finished."

"I can see," he replied, his gaze wandering the ceiling. Then he looked at her. "Carina, don't you ever stop and take a rest? You've been roaming the ship for days, organizing people left, right, and center ever since we got away from the Regian system."

"There's a lot to organize. Someone has to do it."

"Is there really? Don't you think you can trust the Black Dogs to figure a few things out for themselves, like fixing the airlocks, working out a meal prep rota, et cetera?"

Bryce's gaze felt uncomfortably piercing in the soft lights of the dome.

"Uh..." Carina gave a little laugh as she faltered. "I guess so. Just a few."

He squeezed her arm. "Don't get me wrong. Everyone

appreciates what you're doing. But you deserve a break. You could spend more time with the kids, for instance, especially now Parthenia isn't around as much as usual."

"Oh, she's seeing that young merc?"

"Yeah. Kamil Stanton. He seems like a good guy. And I think he's only a year younger than you."

"She's growing up," said Carina, side-stepping the gibe.

Bryce snorted with laughter. "Growing up? You're only three years older than her."

"There's more to growing up than aging," she said. "I lived a lifetime before I joined the Black Dogs, while Parthenia had servants waiting on her. You don't know the half of it."

"No, but I can guess. And that's even more reason for you to have some downtime now and then, huh?"

The idea of not spending all her waking moments doing all she could to safeguard those in her care was appealing, but she wasn't sure she could let go so easily. "I can try."

"Good. I knew you'd see sense."

Bryce glanced upward at the men and women working on the ship's hull, then he took Carina's hand and drew her to the edge of the room, where everything was in deep shadow.

"Now, I don't want you to feel pressured," he said. "I know you're not ready to get married yet, but I want to give you something." He slid a hand into his pants pocket, pulled out a strip of fabric, and handed it to her.

Carina took the strip and angled it toward the lights to see it more clearly. She was holding something like a ribbon, only shorter and made from many threads woven into a geometric pattern. The distant beams reflected from golden and silver threads among other rich colors.

"It's beautiful," she said. "Where did you get it?" She wondered if he'd taken it from the *Zenobia*, Lomang's ship, which had carried many rare and expensive items.

"Nowhere. I made it."

Her eyes grew round. "You *made* it? Or do you mean you designed and printed it?"

"No, I made it. With these." He waggled his fingers at her. "I took threads from other fabrics here and there, and printed some others. But I wove them together myself. It took me months."

"Oh, Bryce, thank you. It's amazing. No one ever made anything for me before." She could feel herself choking up. "Do I put it around my neck?" Through blurring vision, she could see small hook-and-eye clasps sewn into the ends.

As she asked him the question, a long-forgotten memory began to surface.

"Well, before you put it on," Bryce replied, "you need to understand what it is. You remember I told you I'd talked to Jace about mage marriages, before I made my badly timed proposal?"

A guilty twinge hit her. "It wasn't badly timed. I just..." She sniffed. Her simple visit to check on the state of the dome was turning into an emotional roller coaster.

"It's okay. It doesn't matter now." He looked around at the nearby furniture. "Let's sit down."

They walked a few steps to a sofa and sat on it, facing each other, their knees touching. Carina put the woven strip down on her lap.

Bryce's expression was intense as he gazed into her eyes. "Jace told me about a mage tradition that takes place before marriage."

The memory that had begun to manifest in her mind grew stronger.

She was a child again, at home with Nai Nai in the ramshackle, two-roomed hut that had been their home. She'd noticed something her grandmother was wearing and she was asking her about it. Then she recalled the old woman's reply.

"I think I know what you're going to tell me," she said.

"Okay, well, let me finish and we'll see if you're right." He took her hands in his. "Jace said the tradition is, if a mage man wants to express their love for someone, they weave a ribbon for the person to wear, called a love band. If the band is accepted, it means the feeling is reciprocated. Mage women sometimes weave the bands, but it's usually a guy thing. It's not an engagement as such, just a statement of feelings. So I made you that. I was going to give it to you that day on the *Duchess*."

"And I pushed you away," said Carina. "I'm so sorry."

"No, don't be sorry. I already told you we don't even have to get married, but after what Jace told me, I still want to give you the band."

A fat tear welled up in her eye, slipped out, and ran down her cheek. She swallowed. "My grandmother had one of these. She never took it off. I didn't know my grandfather. He died before I was born. I asked her, once, what the band was, but all she would tell me was that I would find out one day. My grandfather must have made it for her."

Another tear slipped out.

Bryce reached up and wiped it away with his thumb. "Isn't that something to be happy about? He must have loved your grandmother very much."

Carina slowly shook her head. "The main reason I asked Nai Nai about her band was because I remembered Ma had worn one around her neck, too. It was one of my few memories of her. I realized just now that when I met her again she wasn't wearing it any longer. Stefan Sherrerr must have taken it from her."

Bryce's expression softened to sadness, and he laid a hand on her arm.

Carina dropped her head forward as she gave in to her grief. One day, she might move on from mourning her mother, but the time hadn't come yet.

Bryce wrapped his arms around her, and she laid her head on his shoulder.

Some time later, when Carina's emotions were coming under her control again, he said, "This isn't going as well as I'd hoped."

"It's not your fault," she replied quietly. Then she asked, "Could you put it on for me?"

He took the band from her lap, and she turned her back toward him. Pushing her hair to one side, he looped the band around her neck and fastened it.

Carina touched her new, woven necklace and faced him. "How does it look?"

"Better now *you're* wearing it."

She smiled and wiped the tears from her face. "Smooth. I like it."

"I mean it," Bryce said.

He leaned toward her, and she met him halfway. As they kissed, she momentarily forgot about Ma, and her family, and the responsibility weighing on her to get everyone aboard the *Bathsheba* to Earth in one piece.

8

Calvaley had been given the all clear by the medics, and now Carina had a difficult decision to make: should she return the Sherrerr admiral to the brig or allow him the freedom of the ship? Putting him back in stasis was out of the question. He'd only barely survived from his previous stint of Deep Sleep, and running even one of the stasis capsules would be a waste of power from the emergency generators. The energy they produced was already taken up by maintaining life support and sanitation systems, computing, comm and scanners, and simply keeping the lights on.

Carina decided to go and talk to Calvaley before deciding what to do with him. She'd assigned him a guard, but she wasn't sure it was necessary any longer. It had been a long time since they'd spoken more than a few words to each other.

When she saw him in the waiting room of the sick bay, she was shocked. The admiral was already an old man, but he looked as though he'd aged another ten years since she'd last seen him. Strictly speaking, this wasn't possible: aging slowed down to an almost-imperceptible rate while in Deep Sleep.

Though Calvaley had been in his stasis capsule for many decades, he should only have aged a week or two at most.

He looked up at her from under hooded eyes as she walked into the room. He was seated at the center of a bench, frail hands gripping his knees. His pink scalp showed through its covering of thin, snow-white hair, and deep wrinkles corrugated his neck and face. He looked fragile and vulnerable, but Carina knew he was a person of high intelligence and great mental strength and determination. He would never have risen so high within the Sherrerr ranks otherwise. She also recalled he believed himself to be of high integrity, justifying the cruel control the clan exercised on the worlds they dominated as 'for the greater good.'

She wondered, now he'd had plenty of time to reflect, whether he continued in his self-delusion.

"Ah," he said, gazing at her with watery, bloodshot eyes, "the young private who stole the Dirksens' secret weapon from Banner's Moon. What can I do for you? You want my permission to visit your boyfriend in the men's quarters again?"

Carina sat down, straight-faced despite his attempt at humor. "I'd almost forgotten our first meeting."

"You had? Perhaps that's not too surprising. I am just a very ordinary old man and not very memorable, whereas you, my dear, you are exceptional. If only I'd been aware just *how* exceptional at the time."

Was he attempting flattery in the hope of gaining her favor?

Calvaley chuckled. "There's no need to look so suspicious, Lin. I was being sincere."

"I didn't come here for your compliments," she said brusquely. "I'll be frank. Now that you're better, I don't know what to do with you. You were my enemy, and maybe you still are. I'm curious. If our roles were reversed, what would you do?"

He took no time to consider, replying reflexively, "If our

roles were reversed, you wouldn't be here now. I would have left you to die in the Dirksen castle. I may have given the order to put you out of your misery rather than leave you to starve to death, but that would have been the extent of my mercy."

Carina was taken aback. "You wouldn't have rescued someone in the pitiful state I found you in?"

"You were—perhaps still are—my enemy. Why would I have saved you?" His look was cold and hard.

At first, she struggled to answer. He had a good point. The Sherrerrs must have known how Stefan was treating Ma and her siblings, yet they'd done nothing. She couldn't have expected better treatment if she'd been recaptured by them. Why should she have saved Calvaley, knowing he was their representative and, if he were given the chance, he would have captured and taken her to them?

Yet, when she'd discovered him near death in the ancient mage stronghold on Ostillon, the threat of his existence hadn't been uppermost in her mind.

Finally, she replied, "Compassion? Sympathy? Kindness? We might have been enemies, but we weren't opposing sides in a battle. You were a fellow human being in need. You'd suffered terribly for weeks and were in no position to hurt anyone. Only a monster could have left you there."

Calvaley's expression softened, and he broke eye contact and nodded. "Only a monster indeed."

When he spoke no more, Carina said, "You told me once that what the Sherrerrs were doing was justified, that they were bringing civilization to the galactic sector, and that the sacrifices made would be worth it in the end. Do you still believe that?"

Continuing to avert his gaze, the old man replied, "To be perfectly honest, I am no longer sure what I believe."

His answer wasn't satisfying. She felt she wanted more from him, something firmer to reassure herself it was safe to allow him his freedom. She couldn't tell if he was remorseful over his previous behavior or if he was only hedging, hoping to exploit her altruism, which he appeared to consider foolish.

She couldn't read him, and she was reluctant to Enthrall him, given his age and ill health. She didn't want to permanently damage his mind. Was her reluctance another example of misguided kindness?

"Perhaps, in order to secure a safe future for my family, you think I should be ruthless like you were?" she asked.

"I am in no position to advise you on what or what not to do."

"I wasn't asking for your advice," Carina retorted. She sighed, frustrated.

Calvaley leaned back and looked her in the eyes once more. "I understand what your dilemma is, but I'm afraid I'm unable to help you."

"Why?" she almost begged him. "Why won't you give me a straight answer? Don't you want me to stop viewing you as a threat?"

"I think the problem is, *you* want to stop viewing me as a threat. You want to do the 'right' thing, the good thing, but your fear of making a mistake is holding you back. You don't want to be responsible for someone coming to harm due to a decision you made."

He narrowed his eyes as he continued, "During my days in my little cell, my access to information was limited, and I wasn't prepared to converse with the three maniacs who were my fellow inmates. I've gleaned some information from the medics about what happened while I was in stasis, but, again, I remain hazy on the details. However, what I *do* know is you, your family, and most of your merc band have survived. Apparently, your choices have been effective so far."

Carina thought of Cadwallader, Atoi, and others who had suffered and died, and thought, *But at what cost?*

"I said before I wasn't in a position to give you advice," said Calvaley, staring intensely at her, "but that isn't true. I was once where you are, Lin. I held the lives of many men and women in my hands, some of whom were close to me. If I am to tell you anything, let it be this: people *will* die under your command. It is inevitable. Yet you must make whatever decisions you have to make and live without regret. Do not waste your time in hesitation and self-doubt. If you wish to succeed in your endeavors, you cannot afford that luxury."

He coughed a little, as if to clear his throat, but then the cough turned into a fit of hacking and retching, attracting the attention of medics in the sick bay. Two of them ran into the room to attend to him. One held a medical scanner against his back, while the other gave him something to inhale.

When Calvaley finally recovered, he looked weaker and older than ever.

"I think we need to take another look at you," one of the medics said. "Come inside for a re-evaluation. One more night in recovery won't hurt."

The ex-admiral stood up, though he remained hunched over, and the medics supported him by his elbows as they guided him into the center.

Carina also stood. Her mind was made up.

"If he's better tomorrow and you discharge him," she told the medics, "he can go wherever he wants. I won't send guards."

9

As she left the sick bay, a notification sounded from Carina's comm, and she ran toward the bridge. The *Bathsheba's* computer had finally recognized their position.

By the time she arrived Hsiao was already there, sitting at the pilot's station, her attention focused on her screen. As Carina entered the bridge, the pilot threw a gleeful grin over her shoulder. "You have to see this!"

Returning her attention to her console, she added, "I'll show you the holo. Take a seat."

Carina settled into the captain's chair, and moments later a starscape holo appeared above Hsiao's projector. She dimmed the bridge lights eighty percent, causing the stars to become the brightest light sources in the room. None of the patterns jumped out at Carina as familiar. The area nearest to her was sparsely populated by perhaps eighty or ninety stars. In the farther regions the density thickened until a blaze of suns blanketed the extreme edge of the holo.

"Pretty," she said. "Now, are you going to tell me where we are?"

Hsiao stood up and walked through the image before pointing at a spot roughly three-quarters of the way down the blanket of white dots. Naturally, the *Bathsheba* was far too small to appear on the holo at its current scale, but the computer had provided a green spot to display her position.

"Oh, really?" Carina had been expecting the pilot to tell her their ship was somewhere within the thinly populated area.

"Yeah, I know, right? Who'd have thought we were traveling through such a crowded neighborhood?" She stepped toward Carina and touched a point of red light. "The coordinates for Earth's system put it here."

Carina stood up. "That's it?" she asked in wonder. "That's Earth's star?"

"Yep!" Hsiao's tone was triumphant. "They called it Sol."

"That's really it?" Carina joined her at the side of the holo.

Hsiao laughed and patted her back. "It *really* is. Assuming the coordinates are correct, of course."

Her pulse thudding through her veins, Carina reached out in the semi-darkness to touch the brilliant spot of red. Her finger met nothing but air, yet a thrill passed through her, sending prickles to her extremities.

How long had she wanted to find the home of mages? How long had she yearned to return there? She couldn't even remember when she'd first thought of the idea, she'd been so young. The notion that Earth was finally within her sights was so incredible it seemed unreal.

And yet...

She looked at the opposite side of the holo, where Hsiao had said the *Bathsheba* was located. Though it was only a few meters away, she knew that the distances represented were many, many light years, which meant more time in Deep Sleep before they reached their final destination.

It was one thing to see Earth's sun in a holo, getting there was another thing entirely.

She returned to the captain's chair and returned the lights to their former brightness. The holo faded in comparison and became a vague block that faintly glimmered.

"What does it mean?" She gestured at the 3-D image. "What scale is that?"

"The largest the computer generates," the pilot replied. "But it's cool to see the ship and Earth in the same picture, right? It turns out the Regians don't seem to have taken us on a direct route to their planet after they hijacked the ship, so we were never seventy-odd years off course. It looks like they wandered around quite a bit."

"They must have gotten lost," said Carina. "They had a lucky break when they hit upon a colony ship full of humans, probably on their way to a familiar backwater planet, but after taking over the ship they didn't understand how to navigate it. They were used to relying on the starwhales' homing instinct, or something like that."

"What I don't understand," said Hsiao, "is how did they live so long on the *Bathsheba* while they were trying to find their way home? The ship's stores don't seem to have been touched."

"It's possible that Regians don't eat after they've reached their adult stage. Some insect species are like that. They only eat during the juvenile stages."

Carina's stomach squirmed as she recalled what the young Regians ate.

As her initial elation all but faded, she went on, "We can't expect the starwhales to push us all the way to Earth."

"No," Hsiao agreed. "That wouldn't be reasonable. Have they indicated when they might leave?"

"According to my brother, they've said they'll take us to a safe place."

All the other mages had tried to speak to the starwhales, Carina included, but none had succeeded.

"A safe place of our choosing, or theirs?" asked Hsiao.

"That isn't clear. But if we can give them a destination, maybe they'll take us there. What information do we have on the nearest systems?"

"Not a lot, and it has to be decades out of date. But take a look for yourself. As you'll see, you have a choice to make."

CARINA WANTED to speak to the Black Dogs and the newly joined members of the band, Mezban's ex-soldiers, before selecting the place where they would try to refuel the *Bathsheba*. But before she approached them, she wanted to mull over the scant knowledge she had.

It was odd that, when Cadwallader had been alive, she'd fought his attempts to be more democratic about the taking of significant decisions aboard the ship. Something in her had changed, and now she was eager to hear other opinions.

Was it because it would have been the lieutenant colonel, not her, who would have borne the brunt of the blame if things had gone wrong? The thought made her uncomfortable. Would she have been so cavalier if their roles had been reversed? Calvaley's comment about her need to act ethically and her fear of the consequences of the calls she made had struck home.

After wandering around the ship, thinking over the new information about local systems, she received a comm from Parthenia.

"Where are you? Dinner's nearly over. If you don't get here soon, Oriana and Ferne will have eaten everything."

"Shoot!" She checked the time. "I'll be there in a couple of minutes. Tell them if they don't leave me something I'll Transport them to the other side of the ship without any elixir and they'll have to walk all the way back."

She began to jog toward the family suite she shared with

her siblings. As she ran, she thought over another decision she had to make—one that had been bothering her since Bryce had given her the love band.

When she arrived at the suite, the dining table was indeed mostly empty of food. It was no big deal. Oriana and Ferne were growing fast and always hungry, and printing more to eat didn't take long. She wasn't even feeling particularly hungry, perhaps because she was nervous about the announcement she had to make.

The children were in happy spirits. Darius and Nahla were bouncing in their seats, their slender attention spans for something as boring as eating already exhausted, and Oriana and Ferne were reciting lines from a comedy vid someone had copied across from the *Duchess's* database. Parthenia's head was down over an interface, probably chatting with Kamil.

Carina reminded herself she needed to invite the young man to dinner soon.

Bryce was also there, she was happy to see. His presence wasn't unusual, especially when he knew she was busy and might not make it back for a family mealtime, though sometimes he didn't make it.

He slept in the suite with Carina—and Darius, and often Nahla, too.

Carina took the seat left empty for her and reached for a serving bowl that still contained a little soup.

"Do you want some more?" asked Bryce. "I can get it for you."

"No, this is fine," she answered, spooning out the last of the soup into her bowl. She picked up the remaining piece of bread.

Oriana and Ferne's comic turn came to an end and they burst into giggles.

Carina dipped bread into her soup, took a bite, and chewed as she waited for their laughter to die down.

"I want to run an idea past you guys," she said before there was a chance for more chatter to start up.

Parthenia lifted her gaze from her interface. "What's that?"

Carina put down her piece of bread and laced her fingers together in front of her bowl. "It's mostly going to affect Darius and Nahla, and," she added, focusing on them, "I don't want you to be afraid to speak up if you don't like it."

Oriana shot a puzzled look at her twin.

"Okay," said Carina, but then a sudden bout of nerves hit her. Was she doing the right thing? Was it too soon for Darius and Nahla?

She pushed through her trepidation.

"This suite contains three bedrooms, right? Parthenia has one to herself, Oriana and Ferne share a room, and Darius, Nahla, Bryce, and I are all squeezed into the third bedroom." She grimaced. "It's kind of cramped, isn't it?"

Bryce, clearly catching on about where she was going, rested his elbow on the table and his chin in his palm, and began to watch her with amused eyes.

"But next door..." Carina raised her eyebrows, heralding the solution to the problem she'd outlined, "...next door is a one bedroom cabin."

Parthenia smiled wryly and looked down at her screen.

"Oh!" said Nahla. "That could be for you and Bryce. And then Darius and I could share a room and we wouldn't be so squashed up anymore."

"Exactly," said Carina, greatly relieved she hadn't been forced to state the proposal herself.

Ferne burst into laughter again and whispered something in Oriana's ear. She pushed him away, chuckling and looking somewhat embarrassed.

"What do you think, Darius?" Carina asked. For a long time, her brother had relied upon her and Bryce for comfort while he slept. She hadn't begrudged the inconvenience for a moment. Both he and Nahla had been through a lot, especially considering they were so young. "If it's going to upset you, we won't do it."

"Uh...No, it's okay." He shrugged as if unconcerned, though Carina guessed his attitude might be at least partly due to a reluctance to look babyish in front of his siblings.

"If you're scared in the night, you can always come to us," she said. "Just..." she glanced at Bryce "...use the door comm first."

∼

THAT EVENING, after tucking in Darius and Nahla and saying good night to the rest of the children, Carina joined Bryce in the suite next door. He'd been taking a shower, and as she closed the door he came out of the bathroom in a robe.

"I like this idea," he said. "Are the two little ones really okay with it?"

"They seem to be," she replied. "We'll find out soon enough if they aren't. They'll let us know if they aren't, that's for sure. But they haven't had nightmares for a while now, so I thought we could try. They're tough little cookies."

"They are, and I hope they're okay." He walked up to her and held her in his arms. "It's nice to have some privacy, for a change."

Carina returned the embrace. They kissed, and soon she felt as though she was melting into him. How long had they waited for this? Passion surged in her as Bryce clasped her even closer.

She recalled the skinny adolescent who had followed her out of the tavern on Ithiya, when she'd been so drunk she'd barely been able to stand, citing his concern for her well being. She also recalled his attempt to steal from her, desperate for money to buy the meds that were keeping him alive. He'd come a long way since then—they both had—and she could hardly reconcile her memory with the strong young man holding her to him.

Her fears and worries melted to nothing, and there was only the closeness and yearned-for intimacy of the moment.

Long minutes later, she said softly, "You know, the first time we kissed, I thought, hmm...he's really good at this."

"You did?" He chuckled. "And what do you think now?"

"That hasn't changed."

Bryce pulled her close again, slipping his hands under her shirt and up the bare skin of her back. He began to kiss her neck, starting at the corner of her jaw and working his way down.

When he reached the love band, he paused. "Do you want me to take this off?"

She shook her head. "Never."

10

————

Carina faced the assembled men and women. Some faces were very familiar, like Halliday's, Jackson's, and many other Black Dogs', while some had been growing in familiarity to her over the weeks the starwhales had been pushing the *Bathsheba* through the cosmos. The latter group comprised Mezban's former soldiers.

Ostensibly, they had joined the merc band, but they sat in their own group. All were male, as Lomang's crew had been. She guessed that on their planet women rarely joined the military. They were large-headed and deep-voiced, and they grew out their beards, grooming them into distinctive styles.

Jace, Bryce, and her siblings sat near the back of the large meeting room, Carina noticed Calvaley was present as well. The old man sat alone in a corner, his arms and legs folded as he watched her closely.

She cleared her throat. "Thanks for coming, everyone. I'd especially like to welcome the new members of the Black Dogs. It's good to have you here without the necessity of trying to kill you."

Her dark-humored quip drew chuckles from the original

Black Dogs, but the soldiers who had worked for Mezban remained stony faced. In his corner at the back of the room, Calvaley frowned deeply.

Carina swallowed and continued. "We've been extremely lucky. Just when we thought we faced another battle with the Regians—one we might not have been able to win—we've had a reprieve. What's more, we also have an unexpected ally: a flock of space-faring creatures who have helped us to get away from the Regians. I don't know exactly why the animals are helping us or for how long, so it's imperative we refuel as soon as possible.

"We finally know our position, and we have information on local systems where we can buy fuel and supplies. But where we should go isn't clear. We're all in this together, and the choice could have wide-reaching, perhaps devastating reper-cussions. Unfortunately, I'm no Cadwallader. I don't have his years of experience. While he might have been able to figure out the best place to go, I want your input before I come to a decision. I asked you here to get your opinions."

One of Mezban's men stood up. His arms were crossed over his broad chest, and he fixed her with an imperious look. "I have a question."

His fellow soldiers were gazing up at him calmly, as if knowing what he was about to say. It seemed he was their unof-ficial representative.

"What's your name?" asked Carina.

"Vasya Rebane."

"Go ahead, Rebane."

"We want to know when Pappu will be released."

"Uhh..."

Lomang's brother had been residing in the *Bathsheba's* brig ever since they'd retaken the ship. Carina assumed he shared the same home planet as Mezban's soldiers, and they clearly held him in some regard if they were asking for him to be set free. Carina had no intention of releasing the man, though she hadn't given his ultimate fate much consideration.

On the other hand, she didn't want to piss off a bunch of trained killers.

"That's a discussion for another time," she said, finally.

"We would like to discuss it *now*," said Rebane, placing both hands on the seat back in front of him, leaning forward, and glaring at her.

Indistinct, angry murmurs rumbled through the Black Dogs in response to his aggressive tone.

Appearing to sense he was skirting dangerous ground, Rebane returned to an upright position and let his arms hang at his sides as he said, "Pappu is not a bad man. It was only that he loved and followed his brother, obeying him in everything. Whatever he did while under Lomang's influence should be disregarded. You can trust him."

His fellow soldiers nodded and turned to Carina for her response.

She recalled the giant's hands on her shoulders, forcing her to her knees, and his long, strong fingers around her neck, squeezing the life from her. Trust him? She wasn't going to do *that* in a hurry.

In the corner of the room, Calvaley's full attention was upon her, his eyes seeming to bore into her soul.

"Meet with me later," she said to Rebane, "and I'll hear what you have to say. For now, we have a more urgent decision to make."

After a second or two of hesitation, he sat down. Neither he nor the rest of his group seemed satisfied, but Carina didn't care. She had avoided the problem for the moment.

"According to the ship's database, three colonized systems are within roughly equal distance from us. We should be able to get what we want at any of them, but the information we have is hundreds of years old and could be wildly inaccurate.

Those of you who worked for Mezban are from this sector. If you know anything about these places, I want to hear it. And anyone else, even if you just feel you have something to contribute, speak out. We don't know how much longer we can rely on the starwhales' kindness. My final choice has to be a good one because it may be the only chance we get to continue our voyage."

Her words had subdued the room to complete silence.

She nodded at Hsiao, who dimmed the lights and opened the first holo.

In the space next to Carina a pair of suns appeared, slowly circling each other. Between them could be seen a huge gas giant, but this was not the object of her interest.

"Aberama 12," she said. "One habitable planet, Kvarken. Point seven Standard gravity, primarily aquatic, with oceans covering ninety-two percent of the surface. Last recorded population seventy-one million. Major exports: fish, seaweed, minerals."

"I've heard of Kvarken," said a voice Carina didn't recognize. "For half of its orbit the planet is in constant daylight. It's only during the other half it experiences periods of darkness."

"Do you know anything else about it?" she asked.

"It has a bad rep," said the man. "My dad was a trader, and he told me never to go there. Said the inhabitants are constantly at each other's throats and you can't trust any of them."

Carina squinted into the darkness, trying to find the voice's owner, but all she could see was black silhouettes of Mezban's men. "Maybe you'll know something about the other planets, too."

The man was silent.

She asked Hsiao to move to the next holo.

"Aberama 8," she said as the original one was replaced by a single G-type star orbited by ten or twelve planets, just visible in the glare of the star's light. "This has two habitable planets, one cold, rocky, and one point three Standard gravity, and the other cloudy and hot, with point eight-five Standard."

"Gog and Magog," said the man who had spoken before.

"That's right," said Carina. "What can you tell us?"

"Magog's the hot one," he said. "The elite there inhabit cloud cities. Everyone else lives on the surface. Dad would mostly buy animal hides and seeds of an indigenous wild plant from them and sell them computer parts. I think they have good manufacturing bases for other goods, though. Gog is barely populated. It's too cold for most crop plants and the population lives in domes."

Carina checked the scarce data she had on the planets, which seemed to chime with what the man had said. Gog's population was listed as a mere two million, while Magog's was nearly one billion. A small population wasn't necessarily a negative—the fewer people who knew about a colony ship preparing for a long voyage the better—but it could mean they might not be able to buy everything they needed. The thick, viscous fluid that filled the stasis capsules contained highly specialized, complex chemicals.

"Anything else?" she asked the anonymous man.

"That's all I know."

She asked Hsiao to bring up the third holo. An F-type star lit up the room.

"Aberama 3," said Carina.

"Aberama got around a bit," growled a voice she recognized as Halliday's, drawing chuckles from other Black Dogs.

She continued, not acknowledging the interruption, "Just one habitable planet here: Justice."

"I don't like the sound of that," Halliday quipped, apparently emboldened by the positive reception his previous joke received.

"Halliday," said Carina over the resulting laughter. She

narrowed her eyes at him as he shifted about uncomfortably in the front row, "unless you have something useful to say, shut up."

She continued in the rough direction of the man who had spoken before, "The guy whose father is a trader, what do you know about Justice? It says here it's a high-grav planet, one point nine standard, population unknown, exports mainly rare and precious metals and gems."

"It's young," replied the man. "Highly volcanic. My dad did good business there, but I remember him saying he was never allowed to go planetside."

Carina wondered why. World governments sometimes made disembarkation illegal due to safety concerns—some planets were largely lawless places. In other cases, the government had something to hide, like human trafficking or illegal gene splicing, such as creating human/animal hybrids. That practice had been outlawed in her native sector, and she guessed that Geriel Sector was probably the same.

Yet the mention of gems had piqued her interest. She intended to pay for what she needed with the remaining ember gems. Lomang had said the precious stones weren't found anywhere else in the sector. Justice sounded like exactly the place that would understand and appreciate their rarity.

But she didn't want to make a decision without further input from others.

She told Hsiao to shut down the holo projector and bring up the lights.

Perching on the edge of a table, she said, "Okay, let's talk."

"No!" shouted Rebane, suddenly rising to his feet once more. "First, you release Pappu, then we talk about other things."

"I told you we would discuss Pappu later," Carina retorted. "Sit down."

He jabbed a finger at her. "You're going to keep him locked

up, no matter what we say. You think you can pacify us with delays and prevarication. You cannot. I have explained to you that our friend isn't responsible for whatever offenses he committed. Now you must let him go."

The Black Dogs were sending Rebane and his companions dark glances. A fight was brewing, and if it occurred, Carina couldn't see a way back from it. The two groups of soldiers would be enemies forever afterward, and the atmosphere on the ship would be riven with tension and enmity.

But she was more angry than apprehensive. The mercs had saved Mezban's soldiers from a horrible death on the Regian planet. That fact appeared to have been entirely forgotten.

What she wanted to do was to throw the lot of them in the brig, or even space them. Such a large number of military men would be a constant danger. But the future, as she saw it, was vague and probably hazardous. She might need every one of Mezban's soldiers before long.

"I shouldn't have to remind you that you're guests on this ship," she said. "I told you I would discuss Pappu's situation with you and I will—later. Then, I will listen to whatever you have to say. You have my guarantee. But not now."

She locked gazes with the man.

Suspense over who would be the first to break eye contact stretched out between them, and the silence grew painful.

Carina sensed it was a pivotal moment: she had to demonstrate complete control or face insubordination and the threat of mutiny forever onward.

Finally, Rebane looked away.

She relaxed, but her triumph was short-lived. Rather than sitting down again as she expected him to, Rebane said something in his own language to the men around him. As one group, they stood up and shuffled out of the room, their de-facto leader at their head.

She mentally cursed. During the murmurings of reaction to

the event, she gave Halliday, Jackson, and some other Black Dogs new orders. The mercs rose and followed in the wake of Mezban's men.

Then she noticed that not all of Mezban's soldiers had left. One man remained, though he looked self-conscious.

"Are you the one whose father is a trader?" she asked.

When he nodded, she said, "What's your name?"

"Viggo Justus."

"Thanks for staying, Justus." She addressed the room. "So, where do we go?"

11

K amil led Parthenia by the hand down a rarely frequented passageway.

"I don't understand what the big secret is," she said. "I've been everywhere on the ship. You can't take me anywhere that's new to me."

Kamil had been excited about inviting her to go somewhere with him after the meeting about the *Bathsheba's* refueling stop, but she wasn't feeling it.

"This place isn't new to you," he replied.

"Then why won't you tell me where we're going?"

He was frustratingly silent.

Parthenia dug in her heels, forcing him to stop, and pulled her hand out of his. "If you don't tell me, I'm not going a step farther."

Kamil turned to face her, looking hurt. "It's only a bit of fun. There's no need to be so uptight."

"I'm *not* uptight," she protested. "Do you really expect me to just follow you wherever you want to take me, the two of us entirely alone? I hardly know you."

Kamil's wounded expression deepened. "Hardly know me? I thought I meant more to you than that."

A pang of guilt hit her. "You *do* mean a lot to me, even though we've only been seeing each other for a few weeks, but think about it from my point of view. You're much bigger and stronger than me, and we haven't passed anyone else for ages. If you wanted to hurt me it would be easy, and you could do it before anyone could get here to stop you."

"Gee, you don't have to take everything so seriously."

Parthenia tutted, even more annoyed. "You don't understand, and I think you don't want to either."

She about-faced and began to walk away.

"It's the *Duchess*," he called out to her back. "I was taking you to the *Duchess*. I thought it would be cool to hang out there. The ship's deserted. No one goes there anymore. We would have it to ourselves."

Parthenia carried on walking.

She heard running footsteps, and Kamil touched her shoulder.

"I'm sorry," he said. "That was dumb of me to make a big thing of not telling you where we were going. I didn't mean to spook you."

She halted. "Thanks for apologizing. I guessed you didn't get where I was coming from. It isn't easy to imagine what life is like for me."

"Why don't you come with me and explain? I would never hurt you, Parthenia. I'm shocked you would even think that."

His gaze was so serious and sincere, she relented and took his hand again. They began to retrace their former route.

"It's nothing personal, Kamil. I have to be like this with everyone. I always have to be extra careful, and that's never going to change, unless perhaps we make it to Earth. Things might be different there."

They passed into the silent, empty Deep Sleep chamber.

The empty capsules, like open, transparent eggs, rose in ranks to the high ceiling, shadowy in the low emergency lighting.

Parthenia gave a slight shudder.

"Creepy, right?" said Kamil.

"It's hard to imagine we spent decades in those things," she said.

"And that everyone we left behind is probably dead."

"You're really great at showing a girl a good time, you know that?"

Kamil laughed and grabbed her shoulder, giving her a sideways hug. "That's me! Here we are."

The Duchess's airlock yawned before them, black and foreboding.

"I'm not sure this is such a good idea," said Parthenia.

"Don't worry. I have a few magic tricks of my own." He stepped into the darkness, and suddenly the ship's lights blinked on.

"She still has power?" asked Parthenia.

"Running on auxiliary, like the *Bathsheba*, I expect."

"But I thought her engines were shot away."

"Her engines, not her emergency fuel tank. Come on, let's explore." He took her hand again.

"Okay, but I'm even more familiar with the *Duchess* than I am the *Bathsheba*," replied Parthenia, remembering the long months she'd spent in cramped conditions aboard the merc ship.

"It's not the same when there's no one else about."

They walked through the narrower passages of the smaller starship until they reached the bridge.

Kamil was right: the ship looked and felt different now they were the only ones aboard. The space looked bigger than she remembered it and it had an eerie, forgotten air.

"I wonder how many battles were fought from here?" asked Kamil.

"Lots, I imagine. Carina would know about some of them, but the Black Dogs were in existence for years before she joined."

Kamil sat in the captain's chair and beckoned Parthenia over. When she joined him he moved to one side and pulled her by the waist, encouraging her to squeeze in next to him.

Wrapping an arm around her, he said, "Do you think you'll ever captain a starship one day?"

"Me?! No, I'm not interested in anything like that."

"What are you interested in?"

"Hmm...surviving and living in safety would be nice."

"That doesn't seem a lot to ask. You don't have any higher ambitions?"

Parthenia sighed. "You asked me to explain why I was so cautious about going somewhere alone with you just now. It's because I'm a mage. That carries implications you aren't aware of." She went on to tell him about her early life, growing up in her father's mansion on Ithiya, and what her mother's life was like—though she didn't go into much detail on that. Then she told him how Carina helped them all to escape, and what the family had endured until her sister had hired the Black Dogs.

"You see, Carina isn't doing all of this because she has some wild, romantic notion about Earth. For us, as mages, reaching it could mean the difference between life and death, between freedom and slavery and torture. You might think it would be great to be able to do what we do, but our lives would be a lot safer if we couldn't Cast, if we lived like regular human beings."

"So, when I wouldn't tell you where I was taking you, you thought I might be kidnapping you?"

"It wouldn't be the first time," Parthenia replied. "The knowledge of our powers seems to drive some people crazy. Carina had kept her ability secret all her life until she met Bryce. She never trusted anyone."

"And you don't trust me?"

A guilty ache settled on Parthenia's stomach. "Don't ask me that. It isn't fair."

"You're right." Kamil apologized, for the second time.

In the ensuing pause, Parthenia thought back to the time she'd spent on the *Duchess*, and the *Zenobia*, and before that, the *Nightfall*. So much had happened since departing the Sherrerr mansion, where her life had been tranquil on the surface, though turbulent and bitter underneath. She was tired of the endless traveling, fighting, and danger, and she yearned for actual tranquility and peace, not the facsimile her father had tried to create.

"I brought you here for another reason," said Kamil. "I mean, as well as to spend time alone with you in a ghost ship."

"*Ghost* ship?" Parthenia looked around the bridge once more. The place did have an eerie vibe. "Thanks for that!"

"Don't worry. I'll protect you from any ghouls or zombies that come our way. In the meantime, I'll tell you my idea."

Kamil removed his arm from Parthenia's shoulders in order to turn sideways and face her. "You know when your sister was telling us about the planets we could visit to refuel, did you have a preference?"

"No, I didn't think about it, to be honest. I have no idea which of them would be best."

"I've a feeling she'll pick Magog. It has a big population and a thriving interstellar trade system, so the *Bathsheba* is less likely to stand out and attract attention. And with so many people living there, we're likely to be able to buy whatever we want."

"Okay, but does it matter? We probably won't even leave the ship."

"We might, if we want to." Kamil looked her directly in the eyes. "I have a suggestion. What do you think about disembarking, leaving the *Bathsheba* and not continuing on to Earth?"

"*Huh?!*" Parthenia sat upright and stared at him.

"We barely survived the encounter with the Regians, and it's a long way between here and the end of the voyage. Who knows what else might happen? We might be attacked again, or the ship could suffer a malfunction and we drift to our deaths in the depths of galactic space."

He put a hand on her arm. "If we stayed on a planet around here, we could make a life together. I hear what you say about the dangers of living as a mage, but if you never do anything of those special things you can do, how would anyone know you're different? Don't you think it's safer to live like that than go with your sister across the stars to an unknown future?

"When I signed up to the Black Dogs I was excited to go on adventures, but I've had my fill of them. And I've found you. We get along pretty well, I'd say, and there's no reason things won't get more serious between us over time."

Parthenia didn't know what to say. Kamil had thrust his ideas upon her one after another, not giving her time to absorb one before he was on to the next.

Disembark the *Bathsheba* permanently?

Leave behind her family?

Give up on safely living as a mage on Earth?

Appearing to see her confusion, Kamil said, "You don't have to give me your answer now. We have plenty of time before they set a course for Earth. Think about what I've said. When we find out where we're going, we'll have a better idea if what I'm proposing makes sense. Maybe I'm being an idiot. I don't know. But it's worth thinking about, right?"

Remaining nonplussed, Parthenia could only nod.

12

H er decision on which planet they would refuel at had been made, and most other things in her life were going very, very well indeed. Carina had slumbered deeply, as though cocooned within a thick, soft, blanket of contentment. She was slowly wakening, vaguely aware she should move and rouse herself, but she was fighting it— clinging on for a few more moments of blissful serenity.

A thudding sound was breaking through the edges of her consciousness. Was it the beating of Bryce's heart, where his chest pressed against her back? No. The thudding was too fast, too urgent. Was it one of the kids banging on the door, wanting to speak to her? Perhaps Darius or Nahla, frightened by a nightmare and needing some comfort?

She forced an eye open and saw the darkened bedroom of her new quarters. A light was blinking on the comm panel on the wall next to her bed, and from her ear comm on the bedside table she could hear the tiny *ding!* of a new message notification.

The thudding noise started up again, resonant and angry.

A sense of alarm filtered into her groggy mind. Whoever

was hitting the door was strong—strong enough to make a noise through the thick material, designed to suppress external sounds.

"Stars, what's that noise?" murmured Bryce as he also woke up.

He rolled onto his back, smacking dry lips and withdrawing the arm that had been wrapped around her, and allowing Carina to slide to the edge of the bed and reach for the wall comm.

She swiped it, and Vasya Rebane materialized on the screen. He looked livid with anger.

"I know you're in there, Lin!" he shouted through the speaker. "Open up! You can't avoid me forever."

Bryce peered at the panel over her shoulder, and rolled away again, groaning, "It's way too early to see that face."

Carina closed the connection and turned to give him a look.

"He could hear me, right?" he asked.

She rolled her eyes and opened the comm again. "Sorry, Rebane. I was asleep and didn't hear the door chime. Give me a minute, okay?"

The man looked fit to burst a blood vessel as he opened his mouth to reply, but she swiped the screen and his face disappeared. Still reluctant to emerge from peaceful oblivion, she pushed down the covers and sat up. She rubbed away the sleep that had gathered at the corners of her eyes, and then reached for the robe that lay across the bedclothes.

As she stretched out, Bryce caressed her back, and the sensation brought back evocative memories of the previous few nights they'd spent together. She turned and leaned down to kiss him, but it was just a quick peck on the lips. Anything longer and she might be too tempted to keep Rebane waiting a long time. Nevertheless, Bryce's hands wandered over her, and it was an effort to move away, swing her legs off the bed and stand up, pulling on the robe and fastening the tie.

She padded across the living area to the door and opened it a fraction.

"I know why you're here," she said quickly, before Rebane could launch into the tirade that lurked behind his furious visage. "I'll meet you in the captain's office in fifteen minutes."

"No! We have waited long enough!"

At his mention of 'we' Carina noticed ten or more of Mezban's soldiers hovering in the passageway directly behind him.

"We *demand* that you release Pappu immediately," Rebane continued, adding as his volume dipped and he leaned in and glared, "or we will release him ourselves."

"You aren't in a position to demand anything," Carina replied evenly. "As I said before, all of Mezban's former soldiers are here at my invitation, and that invitation can be revoked at any moment. We're nearing habitable zones, so if you want to remain in service aboard this ship, I would think about that if I were you. Meet me at the captain's office in fifteen minutes if you still wish to discuss Pappu's situation."

Her gaze not leaving Rebane's, she closed the door.

When he could no longer see her, however, her defiant attitude withered and she trudged back to the bedroom.

"I've been preoccupied with deciding where we should go to refuel," she said to Bryce, who was still lying down, his hands behind his head.

"I'd forgotten about Rebane and his 'demand'," she continued. "I guess I'd better get ready and go and talk to him."

"Come over here," said Bryce.

"I don't know if that's wise," Carina replied, though she obeyed the request.

When she reached him he grabbed her waist and pulled her down onto the bed before kissing her softly and deeply.

She knew she could have lain there and been kissed by

Bryce all day if she'd had the choice, but she didn't. She gently pushed his chest to break away.

"What are you going to say to him?" he asked, his face hanging over hers.

"I hadn't gotten that far yet. All I know is I can't let Pappu out. He can do a lot of damage when he's riled. But I'm not sure how Rebane's going to react when I tell him. Things could get nasty."

"Then don't tell him. Say...uh..." His gaze shifted away from hers and then returned. "Say you have the matter under consideration, or some other bullshit."

"I'd love to, but I don't think it's going to work. You saw how he is right now. He looked like he wanted to rip my head off."

Bryce gently clasped her head. "Noooo! He can't do that. I like it too much."

Carina exhaled deeply and looked into his eyes.

Her new intimacy with Bryce was double-edged: she loved their physical closeness, which had opened up whole new areas of each other to explore, but she also felt uncertain and vulnerable. As well as the anxiety induced by opening herself up to a non-mage, brought on by the warnings Nai Nai had drilled into her with rigid discipline throughout her childhood, she was also consumed by the fear that, if something were to happen to him, it might destroy her. If that were to happen, she didn't know if she would still be capable of protecting her family.

Her relationship with Bryce was stronger than ever, but somehow it had made her weaker.

How Ma must have suffered when Stefan Sherrerr killed her father. She didn't know how the woman had managed to carry on.

"Do you want me to come with you to talk to him?" Bryce asked.

"Hmm?" Carina replied, dragging herself back to her

present predicament. "No, it's okay." Unwillingly, she eased out from under him. "I'll get dressed. If I'm late, Rebane might just explode, or, worse, attack the brig with his buddies."

"Do you think he'd really do that?"

"Yes, and that's something I *didn't* forget about. After he and his cronies left the meeting the other day, I tripled the guard on the brig. If Mezban's soldiers do decide to take matters into their own hands, the guards should have time to get the word out to the rest of the Black Dogs before they're overwhelmed."

She got up, grabbed her ear comm, and padded into the bathroom, popping in her comm as she went. Rebane had left her thirty-one messages. She told her comm to erase them before playing any others she had.

The kids had left a few silly messages that made her smile, and Oriana had asked her and Bryce to join them for breakfast. She would have to leave that to Bryce.

While she was in the shower, she recalled his offer to help her with Rebane. His intentions were kind, but she wasn't sure his presence would help. However, the thought sparked an idea of someone else who might be useful to have on hand, someone much more experienced than either of them, whose opinion and advice Cadwallader had valued highly. She messaged him and, after quickly explaining her problem, asked if he would join her at the meeting.

13

W hen she entered the captain's office, Jace was already there and waiting, along with Rebane. The latter had come along without his entourage of fellow soldiers, she was relieved to note.

Jace and Rebane were chatting, but they stopped as Carina walked in.

She was surprised by the apparent congeniality between the two men. Rebane appeared relaxed, even cheerful. He stiffened at the sight of her, however, and his eyes narrowed with what looked like suspicion or enmity.

"Carina," said Jace, "thanks for inviting me to your meeting. I've been talking to Vasya about his home world. It's been very interesting."

The man's expression softened again.

She looked from one man to the other before replying to Jace, as she sat down, "I'm glad to have you here." Placing her elbows on the table, she continued, "I'll come straight to the point—"

"Before we get to the reason for the meeting," said Jace, "do you mind if Vasya finishes what he was telling me? It'll only take a minute."

Nonplussed, Carina replied, "Sure, go ahead."

The man in question hesitated, then said, "I was telling Jace about a global annual festival we hold on Lotacrylla. In ancient times, it celebrated the return to the regions they inhabited of a migratory animal my ancestors relied on for food. Now the festival is purely a ritual, naturally."

"So the practice you mentioned doesn't involve live animals?" Jace asked.

Rebane smiled and gave a slight shake of his head. "Archaeologists have found great pits filled with bones from the times when a great slaughter and feast would take place, but these days parents make large models of the beasts and fill them with trinkets and candy, and children break them open the morning of the celebration."

· "That sounds like a lot of fun," Jace said. "Don't you think so, Carina?"

"Um, yeah."

"And what do the parents do to celebrate?" asked Jace.

Rebane smiled even wider, baring two even rows of large, white teeth and reminding Carina of the recently deceased Lomang. "What do you think? We get drunk, of course!"

Jace laughed heartily and slapped the man on his back. "I like the sound of this festival more and more."

Carina managed something she hoped resembled a cheerful face, though she was completely confused. Firstly, in all the time she'd known him, she'd never seen Jace take even a sip of an alcoholic drink, so she had no idea why he was faking camaraderie with Rebane on the habit, and, secondly, she didn't understand what any of this had to do with Pappu.

Before she could return the conversation to the subject at hand, Jace asked Rebane, "Do your people have any other customs?"

He pondered before answering, "Nothing universal springs to mind. Lotacrylla has been settled many thousands of years, and our nations have developed discrete identities and customs. Ah!" He raised a finger. "Except for this." He stroked his highly styled beard. "In all the other worlds I've visited, I haven't seen any men wearing their beards as we do. Yours is impressive, but—I don't mean to be rude—it's quite untamed. On my home planet, men take great care over their facial hair. A man would never be seen in public with an ungroomed beard. So I guess you would call that another Lotacryllan custom."

"Lomang was clean-shaven," said Carina. "How come?"

Jace glanced at her, seeming to approve of the question.

"Lomang belonged to the ruling class," replied Rebane. "The practices of ordinary people didn't apply to him."

"Right," Carina said. "I get it."

"And Pappu?" Jace asked gently. "As Lomang's brother, he must belong to the ruling class too? Is that why you would like him to be released?"

A flame of anger flickered in Rebane's face, but it was quickly replaced by resignation. "Pappu is...I'm not sure how to say it...Simple? His thinking is not the same as regular people. He must be told what to do. Now that Lomang is dead, Pappu is no longer dangerous." He addressed his last remark directly to Carina, in a pleading tone.

Now that he'd lost his aggressive, abrasive attitude, and in light of what he'd told her about Pappu, she felt a little more disposed to letting the man go free, but she hadn't made up her mind yet.

"You must know you're asking a lot," she said. "Pappu nearly killed me—twice. He's a walking lethal weapon, and if what you say is true, a single command from someone he respects could result in murder."

Rebane deflated a little. "I don't think he's ever been alone before. He needs company."

Carina recalled the giant sitting at the feet of his brother, listening to Lomang's endless drivel and self-aggrandizing. She also recalled his childlike fear of Mezban, despite his huge size. What Rebane had said made sense, but the notion of Pappu walking around the ship unrestrained filled her with apprehension.

"I'm not going to give the order for his immediate release, but I am going to think about what you've told me. And in the meantime I'll look into ways to make his incarceration more bearable for him."

Rebane spread his hands wide and said, "That's all we were ever asking." He rose to his feet and bowed.

"We should meet up sometime and I'll tell you about Ostillon," said Jace.

"I would like that," Rebane replied, and then left.

Carina leaned back in her seat to watch him until he'd gone some way down the passage.

"That *isn't* all they were ever asking," she whispered to Jace. "You were there too, right? You saw how they behaved."

"You got a positive outcome," he replied, "yet you're still complaining?"

She frowned, frustrated, though she wasn't sure why. Perhaps it was because she didn't understand the transformation Rebane had undergone after leaving her and Bryce's cabin and arriving at the captain's office.

Appearing to sense her bewilderment, Jace continued, "Mezban's men have lost their leader, and they're far from home. They have no history at all with you or the Black Dogs, and so they must feel insecure in their status on the ship. I think Pappu is more than an incarcerated man to them. He represents something—their identity, perhaps—hence their desire to see him released. It's symbolic, in a way."

Her frown deepened. Pappu represented Mezban's soldiers' *identity*? What the hell did that mean?

Jace grinned. "I think Vasya just wanted to be heard, you know?"

"Okay," said Carina, setting aside her confusion for the moment. "Whatever. As long as he's happy for now and we can move ahead with the important stuff. Thanks for coming along, Jace. You were a big help."

"You're welcome," he replied. "Any time."

Carina resolved to honor her promise to Rebane to look into improving Pappu's day-to-day life in the brig, but she wouldn't be reducing his guard, despite her new knowledge of his mental status. She might even increase it. If he was so easily controlled, what might he do under the instruction of someone like Rebane, who had problems with anger management?

"By the way," said Jace, "have you come to a decision about where we're going?"

"Yes," she replied. "Magog."

14

They had to fly the starwhale to the cloud city. Carina wasn't happy about it, but they had no choice. Trying to land the *Bathsheba* on Magog was out of the question: the vessel simply wasn't built for landing anywhere, let alone withstanding the effects of passage through an atmosphere, and, even if they did manage to get her down in one piece, the notion of the ship escaping planetary gravity was ludicrous.

Somewhere in the *Bathsheba's* long history, the shuttlecraft that had ferried her colonist passengers to their new world had been permanently parted from the ship, and the *Peregrine's* and the *Duchess's* dropship fuel tanks were empty—the Regians had been thorough in enacting their revenge. So, if they were to visit Magog, it had to be aboard the starwhale.

Yet landing a living space creature at one of the planet's spaceports would attract a lot of unwanted attention. Carina feared it would be like hanging out a massive sign with an arrow pointing downward and saying: The Colony Ship Owners Are Right Here. Local authorities and non-governmental skywatchers might have already spotted the rare and extremely valuable relic of a former age in their system. Once a galactic sector had been explored and colonized, no one invested in the building of the vast vessels.

Eventually, someone would find the temptation to try to seize the ship too great to resist, and Carina and her companions would become targets.

Her plan was to smoothly navigate Magog's immigration and customs, arrange delivery of the much-needed fuel, perhaps pick up a few desirable items like printer supplies and unprintable products, and then get offplanet as quickly as possible.

Hsiao had come along, having left her new apprentice, a Black Dog called Bibik, at the helm of the *Bathsheba,* though due to the situation his position was honorary only. Carina had invited the pilot in case there was an opportunity to buy a large shuttle, which might come in handy when they reached Earth.

Darius was also aboard the starwhale, much to Carina's regret. She hated subjecting her young brother to the risks of the visit, but he was the only one who could talk to the starwhale, who, for some reason, he'd named Poppy.

Viggo Justus was there, too. Carina valued any input the man might have on the people of Magog, the rules and regulations, and even their culture. She figured local knowledge would help in business dealings. Another reason for including the man on the trip was to appease Rebane and the rest of the Lotacryllans. She'd thought about what Jace had said regarding their 'sense of identity' and, though she thought the whole idea was pretty airy fairy, she hoped her decision would help them feel represented.

For some reason, Parthenia had insisted on accompanying the party, along with Kamil. Carina wasn't sure why, except perhaps, probably like most everyone aboard the *Bathsheba,* her sister was desperate to set foot on a warm, green, friendly world. Without any concrete objection to offer and knowing her Parthenia's thirst for independence and self-determination, Carina had agreed.

As she mentally went over the starwhale's passenger list, she was sitting in the space behind one of Poppy's transparent apertures, watching the approach to Magog.

Hsiao suddenly appeared. "Mind if I join you?"

"Sure." Carina shuffled her butt sideways, making room for the pilot.

"Whoa," said Hsiao as she entered the space and caught sight of the vista beyond the starwhale's visual organ.

Carina knew what she meant. Poppy had already dipped so low that the black of space was only visible at the extremities of the view. A sea of cloud made up the remainder, interspersed with flashes of brilliant, emerald green from the planet surface. Among the clouds, though they were difficult to spot due to the distance, the tall spires of shiny, white constructions poked up. Carina supposed the constructions were supported somehow, but they appeared to float independently, disappearing and reappearing as clouds washed over them like waves across an exposed reef.

"I've never visited a cloud city before," said Hsiao. "How about you?"

Carina frowned, casting her mind back over her time as a merc, when she'd made planetfall on many worlds. "Uh uh," she replied, giving a small shake of her head. "I don't think so. I think I would have remembered something like this." She jerked her chin at Magog.

There was no denying the place was stunning, but, like every planet, it would hold secrets and dangers she could only guess at.

She was about to ask the pilot what suggestions she had for landing Poppy at the spaceport, but Hsiao held up a hand and put the other to her ear.

"Did you get that?" she asked after a few moments of listening.

"No," Carina replied. "What was it?"

"Your comm's still fixed at shipboard frequency," said the pilot. "You need to switch it to Galactic. The nearest spaceport just contacted us—a place called Japheth—do you want me to respond and go through the protocols?"

"Sure. Tell them our ship is the Poppy, out of...Ithiya."

Hsiao nodded assent. "They won't have heard of Ithiya, but we have to give them a name."

She began a murmured conversation with Japheth space traffic control. At one point she chuckled and said, "Yes, she certainly is."

Carina guessed the traffic control officer had remarked upon their unusual vessel.

Hsiao turned to her and said, "All done. We're cleared to land. Should I talk to Darius about where Poppy has to go?"

"Yeah," Carina replied. "Good luck," she added as the pilot climbed out of the cavity.

Hsiao would have to convey the landing instructions to a seven year old, who would then Send them to an alien space creature, who would then have to somehow comply with them, despite the unfamiliarity of the situation. Had Poppy ever landed at a spaceport? The Regians had raided settlements on undeveloped planets, and had probably never even attempted to land a ship at a regular port. Carina hoped their living ship would understand what to do, and she wouldn't come to any harm.

THE MAGOG IMMIGRATION officer's expression was stern as Carina approached her station at Japheth spaceport. A transparent barrier divided her from the tall, blonde woman, whose eyes were blue like Cadwallader's had been.

"Your party has supplied no documentation," said the officer. "Are you its representative?"

"Yes. We're from out-sector."

The woman's eyebrows lifted a fraction. "Out-*sector*?" She lowered her gaze to her screen. "Name?"

"Carina Lin."

Carina had contemplated assuming a fake name, but she couldn't imagine her notoriety would have spread as far as the edge of Geriel Sector, and using false names during the visit could attract attention if they got them wrong.

She glanced over her shoulder at Hsiao, Justus, Darius, Parthenia, Kamil, and Halliday, who stood in a roughly assembled group at the mandated distance of three meters behind her. She'd told the mercs to wear mufti and come unarmed. All were watching the proceedings uneasily.

If they were turned away at Japheth's spaceport it was unlikely they would be allowed in at any other on Magog. They would have to either attempt a clandestine landing and take the risk of operating illegally on the planet, or try their luck at Gog.

"What's your reason for visiting Magog?" the officer asked.

"Business."

The woman lifted her gaze and glared at Carina. "I'm going to need more than that."

"I'm here to buy starship fuel."

"Really?" The corner of her lip lifted sardonically. "I heard about the 'ship' you arrived on. I'm sure someone has some hay or oats to sell you."

"What?" Carina looked over her shoulder again, wondering if the others had heard what the officer had said and could shed some light on what she meant. But they appeared as confused as she felt.

The immigration officer chuckled at her own joke, before turning serious again. "Every member of your party must submit full bio data."

"That's fine."

"Good. You first."

A screen next to the officer's booth slid sideways, revealing a narrow entrance. After a third and final glance at the people accompanying her, she stepped into the stall. The door slid shut. A screen faced her and, above and below, tiny lenses scrutinized her from every angle.

Carina followed the automated instructions to allow the machine to obtain her fingerprints and retinal and breath signatures. Then a slot opened and a small metal tray holding a plastic cup slid out. Words on the screen instructed her to spit in the cup.

Shit!

There could be only one reason the Magog authorities wanted her saliva: the bio data they collected from visitors included DNA. Carina had never knowingly given up her DNA. It was yet another of the prohibitions involved in being a mage. Her abilities were almost certainly encoded in her genes, and allowing a third party access to that information would put her in jeopardy.

A window jerked open, and the immigration officer scowled through it. "Is there a problem?"

"No, er, my mouth's dry, that's all. Long flight. I'm working on it."

"Do that. I don't have all day."

The window slammed shut.

Carina continued to hesitate. If she didn't spit in the cup, she would be refused entry at the very least, but she was more likely to trigger suspicions she was a criminal. She would be detained for who knew how long, and her party would be split up. It would be a disaster. Darius was the only one who could Send to Poppy to get everyone off the planet.

She couldn't even 'change her mind' about visiting Magog and try to leave. That would look just as suspicious.

She was trapped.

Misgivings weighing her down, she leaned forward and spat. The metal tray slid out of sight and the slot closed. At the same time, the door behind her opened.

"You have three days on Magog," said the immigration officer as Carina walked out.

"Only three days?"

Would that be enough time? Carina wasn't sure.

"A Magog day is six hours Galactic," added the woman.

"Eighteen hours! But that isn't—"

"Wait for your party over there." The officer jabbed her thumb, indicating a spot behind her booth.

"I need to help my brother," Carina replied. "He's only seven."

"His instructions will be child friendly. Wait over there."

Did Parthenia and Darius know they weren't supposed to give up their DNA? Had Ma told them? If she had, would they refuse to spit and create a ruckus? She couldn't speak to them before they passed through the immigration screening.

Turning to face her companions, she mouthed *It's okay*, and gave them a double thumbs up. It was the best she could do.

15

Stepping through the exit to Japheth spaceport, Parthenia blinked in the sunlight. But it was more than sunlight that was hurting her eyes. A sea of blinding white surrounded her. The only exception to the color was a pale gray ribbon of road that ran across the exit, disappearing at its extremities into thin, vaporous cloud. A delicate mist wreathed her feet and rendered everything at ground level more than a few meters away indistinct.

In the distance, glossy white buildings rose out of the cloud, some squat, square and flat-roofed while others were taller and culminated in spires, either slim and straight, narrowing to needle points, or tightly twisted and topped by flat platforms.

"Oh," said Darius, covering his eyes with both hands.

"I guess that's what these are for," Hsiao said as she lifted her sunglasses. Everyone in the group had been handed a pair just before leaving the spaceport.

"Yes," said Parthenia. "Put on your glasses, Darius."

"I feel light," the little boy commented as he followed her advice.

"That's because the gravity is lower here than on the

Bathsheba." Parthenia slipped her sunglasses on. The scene dimmed, easing the pain in her eyes, and became more sharply defined. Where the white of the buildings had caused them to appear melded into the clouds that surrounded them, they stood out clearly now. She could see a wide conglomeration of the structures that she guessed indicated the site of the main city, though it was hard to tell how far away it was. Her sense of perspective was confused by the lack of landmarks.

The air was chilly and humid, but it also smelled fresh and clean and very unlike the stale, recycled atmosphere aboard the *Bathsheba*. Parthenia breathed deeply but then shivered slightly and rubbed her upper arms.

Carina was already walking toward the roadside, looking from side to side.

More new arrivals were flooding from the spaceport exit, pushing past her to line up at a sign. The screen bore a message in three scripts. Parthenia could only read the one at the top, which said: Free Transport to Japheth.

Kamil, who was standing at her side, gave her a sideways hug and said quietly in her ear, "What do you think so far?"

"We've only just arrived," she replied. "We don't know anything about the place yet."

He released his clasp on her shoulder, straightened up, and said, "I think it looks spectacular. It must be amazing to live here."

Alarmed at his comment, spoken at normal volume, Parthenia looked with concern at her sister, but Carina didn't seem to have heard him.

Kamil was rushing ahead with his idea of the two of them abandoning the voyage to Earth and settling on Magog in a way that made Parthenia extremely uncomfortable. She resolved to speak to him frankly when they had a moment alone together.

"I guess we wait here," said Carina, indicating the line next to the sign, which was already long. "I'd prefer to hire a car, but we don't have any currency. We only have the gems, and I'm not giving one of *those* over for car hire."

"Is there a problem with taking the bus?" asked Hsiao.

"We're only allowed eighteen hours until we have to leave," Carina replied. "I wanted to save time."

"Eighteen hours isn't long," said Justus, the Lotacryllan man who had known a little about trading in this region of the Geriel Sector.

"You're telling me," Carina said, moving to the back of the line and gesturing for the rest of the group to join her. "We'll just have to do what we can in the time available. Maybe we can conclude negotiations from orbit. I don't want to overstay and attract attention from the authorities."

Especially not now they have our DNA, Parthenia thought as she walked to the line. Mother had always disposed of her and her siblings' hair and nail clippings carefully, and warned them to do the same if they were ever outside the family home. Giving the Magog immigration office a sample of her saliva had felt very wrong, even though Carina had said it was okay.

Minutes later, an autobus arrived. Three decks high and slim, the vehicle glided just above the surface of the road. Parthenia recalled the vehicles on Ostillon had operated in the same manner, without wheels. The Magogians were high-tech, then. They shouldn't have too much trouble buying fuel for the *Bathsheba*.

The line moved forward as the people at the front climbed aboard the autobus. Before long, the bus was full. The doors closed automatically, and it sped away, driverless. The number of people waiting for the next transport had decreased to the group from the *Bathsheba* and ten or twelve others, who seemed to be two families. The children of the families sneaked glances over their shoulders at Parthenia and her companions, somehow able to tell they were different from regular visitors to Magog.

Parthenia looked down at her clothes, which, she had to admit, were scruffy though clean. Everything she'd packed for the trip was similar, too. She didn't possess any better clothes. There didn't seem much point in dressing up aboard the ship, where no formal events took place and you saw the same people day in and day out. Oriana and Ferne entertained themselves with fashion design, but that was only to help pass the time. After the mages had done their meditation for the day, they had to find ways to entertain themselves.

She looked more closely at the attire of the Magogians, and saw it was rich and expensive, reminding her of the clothes in the closets on Lomang's ship, the *Zenobia*. Threads made from precious metals were woven into the fabrics, giving them additional luster in the bright sunlight.

She realized that none of her party were dressed in a style befitting the elite status of the inhabitants of the cloud city, and suddenly her cheeks turned hot with shame. Though she knew it was an instinctive reaction, borne of years of her father's domineering obsession with appearances and flaunting his wealth, she couldn't help her feelings. She yearned to disappear into the ground, except here that would probably entail falling hundreds of meters to her death.

Kamil leaned close and whispered, "Is something wrong?"

"It's nothing, but...We aren't dressed for this."

A Magogian child's wide-eyed gaze was fixed on her as she spoke. The child's mother noticed and jerked the boy's hand, causing him to turn his face forwards.

"Yeah, I see what you mean," said Kamil. "We're gonna stick out like bog fireballs."

"Like what?"

"Fireballs in marshland. You get them when the methane catches light. You can't really see them during the day, but at night they shine out like lamps. They're blue. Quite pretty, actually."

"Well, I don't think it's going to help our cause to be so noticeable," said Parthenia.

"It's unavoidable when you go to a new world," Kamil replied. "Different places have different styles, food, customs. Heck, people even *smell* different. The locals can tell tourists from a klick away."

"Here comes another one!" Darius yelled excitedly as another transport emerged from the mist and glided along the roadway toward them.

"C'mon little fella," said Halliday as the vehicle drew to a stop. "I'll help you up."

The merc bent down to pick up Darius, but the boy protested, "I can do it myself."

Halliday raised his eyebrows and chuckled. "I'll take your bag, then."

He picked up Darius's small holdall and moved out of the way to allow him to step up onto the bus.

Parthenia noticed Carina's deeply worried expression as her sister also climbed aboard. It was hardly surprising. They had to find a starship fuel vendor and negotiate the purchase and delivery of the fuel in a very short period of time. Their task was fraught with danger. Carina would be paying for the fuel with one or more of the ember gems. What if the stones were unknown in this region of Geriel Sector and held no value? Or, worse still, what if their value was known but an unscrupulous merchant decided to simply steal the gems? As offplanet visitors, would they have any recourse to justice?

Parthenia was last to board the bus. Kamil held out a hand to help her up, though she didn't really need it. His face was a total contrast to Carina's. He looked happy and hopeful, as if he were about to embark on a new, exciting adventure.

A sense of shadowy foreboding settled on her. She faced a big decision, and whichever choice she made, she was going to hurt someone.

16

Traveling aboard the autobus from Japheth spaceport into the city brought back memories of Carina's ride to Langley Dirksen's mansion on Ostillon, after Commander Kee had captured her aboard the Sherrerr shuttle. The vehicle maintained the same smooth, a-grav motion. Magog was clearly an advanced world, but on Ostillon that had been due to the Dirksens' exploitation of the rest of the population. She didn't doubt the same was true here, that the elite took advantage of the poorer sections of society. She wondered what conditions were like on the surface of the planet.

She took off her sunglasses, turned in her seat, hanging her elbow over the back, and said to Justus, "You said your father used to trade for animal skins and seeds here. Can you remember anything else he said about Magog?"

"I've been wracking my brains the entire trip," the Lotacryllan man replied. "I want to help if I can, but I haven't spoken to my father for years. Those things I told you were from when I was at high school. The old man would like to bend my ear about his voyages when he got home. I'm sorry to say I never listened closely. I used to find his stories boring. You know what teenagers are like. The only other comment I remember him making is he could never seem to make a good deal here. He always came away barely breaking even. I think after a few tries he gave up and never came back."

"Ugh," Carina said, "that doesn't bode well for us. *If* I can find someone to sell us some fuel, I might just have to pay whatever price they ask."

She faced forward and watched the shifting cloud scenery and approaching buildings as the autobus skimmed the roadway leading to Japheth City.

Hsiao, who was sitting ahead of Carina on the left-hand side of the autobus, began talking to one of the locals, a skinny man with protruding cheekbones, dressed in a formal, pale blue suit, the jacket ending at his knees. The pilot was asking him about the infrastructure that supported the city.

"It's quite a complex system, but basically most of what you can see floats upon helium balloons. In order to maintain a steady height, the gas is added or released to counteract fluctuations in local air pressure and currents. There's also a degree of flexibility in every construction to allow for movement. To keep the city in one place, giant tethers run from the base to the ground below."

"I was about to ask about that," said Hsiao. "So, there's no way of moving the city, or parts of it, to another place? I was thinking that propellers or jet engines could move places like this quite easily."

Carina smiled, imagining the pilot must be fantasizing about flying an entire metropolis.

"I believe in the early days of the cloud cities, hundreds of years ago, some attempts were made," the man replied, "but the stress on the constructions was too great. A number of tragic accidents occurred. Nowadays, attempting to move a cloud construction is illegal."

Hsiao looked disappointed.

The road suddenly dipped and the surrounding cloud disappeared. They were traveling along a road bordered by villas. Flat, green lawns ran from the road to the fronts of the houses. Most had steps leading up to a veranda, overhung by a pitched tile roof. On the driveways sat torpedo-shaped vehicles, their rounded, wheel-less bases resting directly on the ground.

The bus slowed down and halted, and the man in the blue suit alighted with his wife and kids. Carina guessed the locals had some way of comm'ing the vehicle to tell it to stop. The family was the last of the Magogians to depart. Now, the bus only contained the group from the *Bathsheba*.

As neither she nor any of her companions had access to the vehicle's system, they would have to wait until the bus reached the end of its route.

It arrived sooner than she'd thought. The autobus veered sharp left and glided downward, following a new road that ended in the large, dark mouth of a tunnel. Before Carina even had a chance to decide whether they really wanted to go that way, they'd entered the tunnel. Lights on the walls scudded past.

"Where are we going, Carina?" asked Darius.

She didn't reply, but leaned forward anxiously. The bus was speeding up. Why was it doing that? Maybe they should have gotten off the last time it stopped. The local man hadn't said anything, but there could be all kinds of reasons for that.

Then a sudden burst of light nearly blinded her, and the bus braked and halted. She put on her sunglasses. The vehicle had emerged into a wide plaza, open to the sky. Shops and cafes ringed the space, which was bustling with pedestrians.

"This must be the end of the line," Carina said, sliding out of her seat. She lifted her bag onto her shoulder and went to the exit.

The group climbed down from the bus and out into brilliant sunlight and the noise of the crowd.

They were standing on a sidewalk several meters wide that ran around the inner circumference of a circular, one-story, open air mall. The now-empty bus pulled away and slipped seamlessly into the flow of vehicles that sped past. The cars were similar to the one Carina had seen before: a-grav, tube-shaped, and flawless. They stopped to drop off and pick up shoppers at the curbside before zooming off again, clearly controlled by an autonomous traffic system. The central area beyond the road appeared to lack a floor—hazy cloud billowed up, obscuring the view of whatever lay beneath.

"Where to now?" Halliday asked. The merc was still carrying Darius's bag for him.

Carina didn't know. People were flowing around them like a river around rocks. The Magogians chattered, laughed, gossiped, and exclaimed, all seeming happy and in high spirits. They also appeared to be rushing, however, and Carina wondered why until she remembered that a day and night on Magog only lasted six Galactic hours. That probably didn't allow much time for shopping or leisure activities. She looked up and saw that the sun had already moved a significant distance across the sky during their short journey from the spaceport.

"Let's go over there," she said, noticing a spot that didn't look quite so busy. She pointed toward it and forced a passage through the crowd, fighting against the current of bodies.

When she reached the area the reason for its comparative emptiness became clear: a silver plaque stood there at a ninety degree angle, surrounded by low railings. Names were inscribed on the plaque below the title, Mayors of Japheth.

Unless they stepped over the railings, which probably wasn't allowed, the space was just as crowded as everywhere else. Carina checked the other members of her party had caught up to her. They clustered, buffeted by passing pedestrians.

She felt like screaming in frustration. This was impossible. They had no local money or any means of getting any, and without creds they were cut off from the networks that would allow her to find a starship fuel vendor. Time was also quickly running out. How long had they been there already? An hour? The sun would set soon and they had nowhere to stay, though perhaps that wouldn't be too much of a problem. She assumed Magogians' physical needs were basically like other humans', and they slept roughly eight hours out of twenty-four. That had to mean everything didn't shut down at night.

"Carina," said Darius, tugging on her sleeve.

"Yes, sweetheart?"

"I need to pee."

She let out a sigh of exasperation, but then rubbed his hair affectionately. "Okay, let's find a cafe. I'm sure they'll let you use their restroom."

She scanned around.

"I can see one," Parthenia said.

After another fight to push through the crowd, they arrived outside an eating establishment. Small tables and seats dotted the area in front of the door, and each place was filled. The people sipped drinks and leaned close to hear each other above the hubbub. As Carina approached with her companions, there was an almost-comical sweep of heads turning in their direction. After briefly checking out the newcomers, the cafe's patrons returned to their conversations.

She took Darius by the hand, told the others to wait for her, and stepped through the entrance. Inside, the noise of the street faded a little, and the bright glare of the sun was filtered by something in the glass of the windows. Though the material was entirely clear, the light level was dramatically decreased.

The Magogian customers reacted to Carina and Darius's arrival in the same way as their outdoor counterparts. The conversation instantly dropped to silence but then resumed so quickly Carina was left wondering if she'd imagined the interval. Smartly dressed men and women were crushed into the confines of the space, leaving only a narrow trail through the tables to the service counter.

Only the cafe's human server was paying her any attention, though she had the impression that everyone else was studiously *avoiding* looking at her and her brother.

She navigated the room, Darius trailing, until she arrived at the counter.

"Welcome," said the server, a young woman wearing neat, black overalls. Like the immigration official, she was blue-eyed and blonde. An aura of frizzy hair bushed out all around her head.

The server's gaze flicked to Carina's feet and returned to her eyes. "We're a little busy right now, but if you'd—"

"We actually don't want a table," Carina said. "My brother needs to go to the bathroom. Is it okay if he uses yours?"

"Oh, sure," the woman replied. "Help yourselves. It's right through there." She indicated farther into the cafe with a nod of her head.

"Darius," said Carina, "can you manage to find it by yourself?"

"Uh huh," he replied, and trotted away with some haste.

"This is probably going to sound weird," Carina said to the server, "but I'm looking for somewhere I can buy fuel for a colony starship. Can you help me?"

"*Starship fuel?!*" The woman laughed. "I get some pretty strange requests in this job, but that one tops the lot."

"Maybe you could look up suppliers on your local network? You see, I just arrived, and..." Carina's attention had been drawn by something happening outside the cafe. A few of the locals were talking to her companions. They were not regular shoppers, however. They looked like officials of some kind.

Parthenia and Justus were speaking to them, apparently answering their questions.

Carina's alarm bells went off. What were her sister and the Lotacryllan man telling the Magogians? They weren't doing anything illegal, but, considering their group contained three mages, they had to be extremely careful.

She looked in the direction Darius had gone and then back out into the street, torn by conflicting concerns. She didn't want to leave her brother alone, but neither did she want the conversation going on outside to continue unchecked.

The server leaned over the counter to see what she was looking at. "Oh, that's the Mayor's Watch. They'll be able to help you."

Suddenly, Parthenia broke away from the group and stepped to the door. As it slid aside, she peered in, quickly found Carina, and said, "Is Darius ready to leave? These people are going to take us wherever we want to go."

Carina urgently motioned for her sister to come closer.

Appearing puzzled, Parthenia walked between the tables to reach her.

"What's going on?" Carina fiercely whispered in her ear, acutely conscious of the server's gaze upon her and the distinct possibility the patrons were trying to listen in, too. "Who have you been speaking to? What did you tell them?"

Parthenia's mouth fell open, then she said, "I was *trying* to help. Those people came up to us and explained they're guides for offplanet visitors. We told them what we needed and they said it wouldn't be a problem. Except *you* seem to think it is," she finished, accusingly.

"Guides for offplanet visitors? Do they look like guides to you?"

Parthenia looked back at the five members of the Mayor's Watch. "You think they don't? What are guides supposed to look like?"

The attention their conversation was attracting made Carina even more uncomfortable. She wanted to tell her sister she needed to be way more discreet, they had to be as anonymous as possible, and she shouldn't have to remind her about it, but she knew it would only make things worse.

At that moment, Darius skipped from the rear of the cafe and grabbed her hand.

"Well?" Parthenia asked. "Are we going with the guides or not?"

Dammit!

Carina felt forced into a corner. If they didn't go with the Mayor's Watch, it would seem strange and suspicious, and she had no clue how she was going to buy starship fuel otherwise.

Yet she had a strong feeling this new turn of events wasn't to their advantage, and the men and women waiting outside were not who they claimed to be.

17

The transportation the Mayor's Watch used was a wide vehicle that came up to Carina's shoulders. Its exterior looked like it was made from burnished steel, and the front and back of the vehicle narrowed down to snub-nosed points. It hung suspended a few centimeters above the road surface, and when one of the Watch opened the passenger door, the large car wobbled.

"Climb in," said the man. "Plenty of room inside."

Watchful and worried, Carina peeked into the vehicle before being the first to enter it. Nothing seemed amiss. Seats covered in thick, soft, deep purple fabric lined the interior, arranged to face inwards.

She chose one of the seats nearest the door and perched on it in a state of readiness, though in reality she wasn't sure what difference her position in the car would make. If the trouble she anticipated occurred, she would need to get everyone out, not only herself.

Still, when Darius was next to step in, she gestured for him to sit next to her. Parthenia stooped as she followed him in, accompanied closely by Kamil. Halliday and Justus took seats on the opposite side from Carina, and Hsiao sat next to Darius after climbing into the vehicle last.

Only three of the Mayor's Watch joined the party from the *Bathsheba*. The other two remained outside when the car door silently and gracefully slid closed. The vehicle rose higher and sped off.

Carina studied their new companions, sizing them up. They all wore figure-hugging, deep red suits comprising jackets that ended just above their hips, matching vests, and straight-legged pants. Slim boots of red leather rose high above their ankles, fastened by gold buttons on the inner sides. Their look was attractive and expensive, and not particularly military, which was somewhat reassuring but not sufficiently so to make Carina relax her guard.

One of the two men in the triad reached out a hand to her, smiling confidently. "I'm Ronny." He'd correctly guess she was the leader of the group.

Carina shook his hand. "Pleased to meet you, Ronny." She wasn't going to tell him her name if she could help it. She had a feeling he already knew it, and she regretted her lapse in security at the spaceport. She should have thought up a fake name for everyone. She'd been too nonchalant and careless.

"This is Malte," Ronny added, gesturing toward to the other man, "and Vasn." His gaze turned to the female member of the Mayor's Watch, who also smiled, though Carina detected a certain frostiness.

All three of them were physically fit, their muscles outlined in the fabric of their suits. *Guides? More like guards*, Carina thought. They didn't appear to be armed, at least.

She still didn't volunteer her name. To avoid the embarrassment of the omission, and fearing one of her own party would feel obliged to tell the Watch all their names, she said, "We don't have much time before we have to leave Magog, unfortunately, and I need to arrange some business in the little time we have."

"I understand completely," said Ronny. "Your sister here filled us in." He focused his grin on Parthenia.

Sister? What else had Parthenia told them? Carina glared at her, but she was whispering with Kamil and didn't notice.

"You'd like to speak to someone about purchasing some fuel?" Ronny said. "It's a shame we won't get the opportunity to show you more of Japheth and Magog, but we're taking you to a dealer who'll definitely be able to help you."

"Is it usual to offer services to visitors like this?" Carina asked rather coldly. "I've never encountered this level of friendliness in all the planets I've visited."

"I can understand it might feel unfamiliar to you—Geriel Sector isn't the friendliest place in the galaxy—but, on Magog, hospitality is an important part of our culture. I was surprised you weren't made aware of the Mayor's Watch at the spaceport. Frankly, it's a little embarrassing for us. I hope you'll allow us to make it up to you over the next few hours."

Carina frowned. "Sure."

She didn't believe him for a minute. What he was saying was completely at odds with the reception they'd received from the immigration officer. Something had happened since they'd left the spaceport that had warranted them being 'Watched'.

The vehicle had left the mall area and was speeding along another road lined with villas, similar to the one the spaceport transport had taken. She wondered how large Japheth was and wished she'd done more research before picking it as the place to land. Beyond the villas hung the ever-present clouds, drifting across the sky. Above, the heavens were deepening to dark blue as night swiftly approached.

Carina leaned her head against the window and peered

upward, wondering which, if any, of the stars was the *Bathsheba*. She already missed Bryce. She'd left him in charge, along with Jace. She hoped the Lotacryllan men wouldn't try anything while she was gone.

"Are we nearly there?" asked Darius, swinging his legs.

Did he need to pee again? His bladder seemed to be the size of a pebble these days.

"Just another couple of minutes," said Vasn, attempting another smile, though it resulted in another frosty grimace.

Darius looked at her and edged closer to Carina, wrapping his arm around hers.

Hsiao, who had been looking out into the cloud cover, suddenly gasped. Carina turned to look in the same direction and saw open sky. The clouds had disappeared, and, for the first time since they'd landed, the ground was visible, far below. In the deepening twilight, she could just make out treetops descending a mountain slope before spreading to the horizon, and an expanse of black water.

"Oh," said Parthenia, "we've left the road."

Carina stared downward. Empty air was all that stood between them and the planet surface.

"Don't be alarmed," said Ronny. "We're only taking a short cut." He winked and continued, "Special privileges of the Mayor's Watch."

"Are the vehicles in Japheth all required to travel on road-ways?" Hsiao asked.

"Yes," replied Vasn. "It's a safety feature, just in case the a-grav cuts out, though that's never been known to happen. If it did suddenly die, the vehicle occupants would only experience a drop of a few centimeters to the road. If we were to lose a-grav out here, on the other hand, something quite different would result."

"No kidding," Carina muttered. It was hard to estimate, but she guessed they were about one klick high. "You know," she said to the Mayor's Watch officers, "I hate to be a party pooper, but I'm really not comfortable with my—" she'd been about to say family and friends, but stopped herself, "with my companions and myself taking unnecessary risks. I'd prefer it if we could stick to the road system."

"Ah, I'm afraid to reach the place we're going, we have to skip outside Japheth City," said Ronny. "It's unavoidable, but we'll be sure to take the safer, though longer, route on your return."

Carina mentally cursed. Where the hell were the Watch taking them? It was clearly somewhere difficult to leave. At least they had elixir with them, and, if the worse came to the worst, they would be able to Transport everyone out of there.

"So, you're taking us to a fuel dealer?" she pressed.

"Yes," Ronny replied, "but the person you're going to see deals in many products and services. Starship fuel is only one of them."

"Cool," said Kamil, his intense conversation with Parthenia lapsing for the first time since they'd set out. "What's it like living on Magog? Seems like a great place."

Parthenia rolled her eyes. Carina wondered if the couple had been quietly fighting.

"To be fair, none of us has ever lived anywhere else," Malte replied, casting a brief glance at his companions, "but, speaking for myself, I love it. Life's easy here, the cost of living is low, and there's plenty to do. Cloud surfing, planet diving, and so on. I doubt there's anywhere better to live in the whole region."

Kamil elbowed Parthenia. She immediately elbowed him back so hard he winced.

Finding their lovers' quarrel tedious, Carina pivoted in her seat to look in the direction they were heading.

Night had fallen. They'd left the clouds behind entirely, and the inky blackness of space filled her vision. No street lights from Japheth or the landscape below lessened the brightness of the stars.

She blinked. Some of the pinpricks of light representing ten thousand distant suns seemed to have formed into a regular pattern of vertical and horizontal lines. She blinked again and realized she was looking at artificial lights shining out from a structure hanging in midair.

"Just another minute and we'll be there," said Ronny.

Carina pushed a hand into her pocket and touched the ember gems she was carrying there inside a cloth pouch. The small stones felt smooth and reassuring. Her other hand gripped the elixir canister strapped to her waist.

The final moments of the journey were completed in silence.

A square entrance to the structure they were approaching opened, spilling light into the darkness. The vehicle flew inside and gently settled to the floor.

They were in a bay that held several more a-grav cars, though they were larger and grander than the Watch's.

Ronny was listening to a message from his ear comm. The car doors opened on each side.

"Our host is ready for you," Ronny announced. "He's looking forward to meeting you very much."

Carina held Darius's hand and climbed out of the car. The hatch that had opened to allow them in automatically closed, shutting out the vast night sky.

She moved away from the vehicle to give the others room to come out.

Pressure on her hand from Darius made her look down at her brother. He gave her a look of encouragement, as if he sensed her disquiet and was trying to make her feel better.

A set of steps led up from the parking bay to a platform bordered by a railing. In the wall next to the platform stood a door, and at the exact moment Carina's gaze fell upon it, the door opened.

Raising his hands above his head as he moved, a tall man strode out and stood behind the railing,

"Welcome, my dear fellow mages," he said. "Welcome to Magog!"

18

Things were a lot quieter aboard the *Bathsheba* without Carina, Parthenia, and Darius around. Bryce had moved back into the family suite in case Nahla's nightmares returned, though she seemed to be coping okay without her little brother for company in her room during the quiet shift. During the active shift, she was busy immersing herself in the mage documents, the ship's database, and any other source of knowledge she came across. The latter included Jace, whom she questioned as closely about mage history and lore as if she were a detective trying to solve a case.

It was at dinner times that everyone appeared to particularly feel the absence of the three missing siblings, Bryce had noticed. Now it was only Oriana, Ferne, Nahla, and himself eating together, the flow of conversation was slower and intermittent. The twins would bicker and tease each other, Nahla would relate whatever new information she'd discovered that day, and he would tell the children if anything interesting had happened aboard the ship—a rare occurrence. Then the silences would come. They were not uncomfortable, however. It was just that they all were alone with their thoughts.

Part of the problem was there was little to do except wait for the excursion party to return with the fuel. It was after that the real adventure would begin.

One dinner time, while Bryce was thinking over the upcoming voyage and wondering what Earth might be like, Nahla said to him, "Oh! I forgot to tell you, Jace asked if you wanted to go to his cabin later."

"He did?" Bryce replied, unsurprised the mage hadn't simply comm'd him. The older man rarely used technology if he could avoid it, and as Bryce wasn't a mage, he hadn't been able to Send to him. "Thanks for the message. I might do that. Will you guys be okay putting yourselves to bed?"

"Ugh, of course!" Ferne exclaimed. "We're much too old to be put to bed. And, besides, if we need a bedtime story we can always ask Nahla."

The little girl grinned at the compliment. "I *can* tell you a story, if you like. I learned a new one today, about a mage family in the olden times who helped other mages escape persecution."

"Did Jace tell you it?" asked Bryce.

"No. I found it in the documents. I told Jace about it."

"Cool," Oriana said. "We'd like to hear it, wouldn't we, Ferne?"

"Sure," he replied.

The twins were wearing matching his and her outfits of brilliant green. Ferne wore a jumpsuit that fastened at the front and a matching jacket that only reached to his waist and elbows, and Oriana wore a dress that hung straight at her sides and reached the floor. Both twins also wore head decorations in the shape of fans, pinned to the backs of their heads. Oriana had recently had her hair cut short to match her brother's at the *Bathsheba's* automated hair salon.

Their clothes were among the strangest they'd ever created, but Bryce had complimented them as he always did. Their activities alleviated the pervasive boredom, no doubt, and helped them develop their creativity.

Though he'd never mentioned it to Carina, Bryce sometimes felt she and the rest of the mages focused too much on the aspect of themselves that set them apart from other humans. Considering how much their magehood impacted their lives, it was understandable, but he worried that it meant they would always distance themselves from regular people. That would be wrong and unwise. Normal people were not their enemies, no matter what Carina's grandmother had taught her or what she'd then taught her siblings. He felt sure the way to safety and acceptance for mages wasn't to live separately from non-mages, keeping their powers secret. It was to be open about what they could do, and to be friendly. Then, if some unscrupulous person tried to take advantage, they would have plenty of ordinary friends to protect them. Mages' clandestine ways had contributed to their troubles, in his opinion.

He scraped the last forkful of beans from his plate and ate them.

When he'd finished eating, he didn't get up from the table right away. He watched Oriana, Ferne, and Nahla as they continued with their dinners. He was glad Carina had chosen to not take them with her.

The fact was, he loved them. He loved Carina, of course, but he loved her entire family, too, and it would have hurt him to not see any of them ever again, or even for a while. At some point during the time he'd spent helping them to escape from monstrous Stefan Sherrerr, and all the later escapades, the children had taken the same place in his heart as the blood siblings he'd been separated from on Ithiya.

He felt especially close to Nahla, perhaps because, like him, she was a non-mage, and also perhaps because she'd suffered the worst of all the family. The mage brothers and sisters always had each other, but for a long while Nahla had only had her psychopathic, sadistic brother as a companion. And then that time she'd seen the pilot killed and been trapped with his dead body...Bryce suppressed a shudder.

The three children had finished their dinners. They piled up their empty plates, along with Bryce's, and Oriana took them to the recycling chute.

"I guess I'll go and see Jace," said Bryce, standing up.

"Can you ask him if he'd like me and Oriana to make him some new clothes?" Ferne asked.

"Yeah, I can do that," Bryce replied. He'd turned down the same offer himself only a couple of days before and felt a little guilty about it, but the twins' creations were not quite his style. He didn't think Jace would be interested in sporting a bright orange gown emblazoned with stars, or whatever it was they would dream up for him, but he would ask.

"See you later, guys," Bryce said as he left. "Don't stay up too late."

Jace lived by himself in a cabin near the twilight dome. Bryce knocked on the door, not knowing if the older man had even activated his comm.

There was no answer.

Then, just as Bryce was about to knock again, the entrance slid open.

Jace was rising to his feet from a position on the floor in the center of his small room. "Sorry, I was meditating."

"I didn't mean to disturb you," said Bryce. "I can come back later, or tomorrow, if—"

"Please come in," Jace said. "It's no disturbance. I was expecting you."

Bryce stepped into the cabin, and immediately halted in surprise. The wall that had been obscured from his position in the doorway displayed a forest scene. He could also hear birdsong and the sounds of other wild creatures and insects.

"Do you like it?" asked Jace.

"It's fantastic. I didn't know it was possible to do that. Do all the cabins have that capability?"

"I don't know. I only discovered it the other week myself. I would have thought they do. There's nothing special about this place."

Bryce was entranced by the scene on the wall, which wasn't a still image. The trees moved and as he watched, a bird flew out from a tree.

"I can set all the walls to the same display," Jace said, "but it's overwhelming, and, to be honest, it makes me homesick for Ostillon."

"You used to be a forest ranger, right?" asked Bryce. He looked around for a place to sit down. The rest of the room was tastefully decorated in a distinctive style. Jace had covered the tile floor with a mat that appeared to be woven from natural materials, though Bryce guessed he must have printed it. A bedspread decorated with vines and leaves lay over the bed, and a very low table sat next to a wall, with two similarly low chairs on each side.

Jace lifted the table and put it down in the middle of the room. Bryce helped by transporting the chairs while Jace collected a tray carrying a jug and two mugs from a corner. When Bryce sat down, he was only a few centimeters above the floor and was forced to cross his legs. As Jace also sat in the same position, he realized that was the idea.

"Can I interest you in a traditional mage drink?" asked Jace, lifting the jug.

"As long as it isn't elixir."

Jace chuckled. "Have you tried it?"

"I snuck a drink one time when Carina wasn't looking. That stuff's pretty disgusting."

"You get used to it. This tastes a lot better."

"I'll have some," said Bryce. "What's it called?" he asked as Jace poured a pale green liquid into a mug.

"Cha," Jace replied. "It's supposed to be very good for you."

He slid the mug across the table to Bryce, who took a sip. The taste was bland but not unpleasant. "It's nice. How did you make it?"

"Surprisingly, the ship's printers have it as a set option."

"They do?" Bryce paused, puzzled. "I wonder why."

"I've been wondering the same myself."

Bryce took another sip.

"How are things going with Carina?" asked Jace.

"Pretty good. She really liked the love band. Thanks for the tip." Bryce considered a moment. "Well, at first it made her cry, but she liked it in the end."

The mage's features softened with sadness. "I didn't think of that. It must have conjured up some bad memories for her."

"Yeah, pretty much, but it was okay once she got her feelings out."

"I'm glad. She's gone through a lot. Is she doing all right generally?"

"You know her. She's doing her usual thing of biting off whatever life throws at her, chewing it up, and spitting it out. Is that why you asked me here?"

"Yes. I worry about her. But she's so independent, she won't tolerate much 'interference'. It'll just make her push me away. She's gotten better recently, but..."

"I know what you mean, but, like you said, I think she's calming down a little now."

"I hope so."

Suddenly, agitated banging came from the door.

Jace gazed at Bryce in surprise before climbing to his feet and walking to the door.

When he activated the manual control, the opened doorway revealed the old man, Calvaley, scowling.

"Your comm is broken," he said angrily. "I tried to hail you several times."

"I apologize," replied Jace. "It isn't broken, only—"

Calvaley pushed past him and strode into the room.

"...turned off," finished Jace, staring at the man's back.

The former Sherrerr admiral turned to face both men. His health appeared to have improved considerably since Bryce had brought him out of stasis. His withered cheeks were tinged pink and his hooded eyes shone, though it was with ire.

"Someone needs to do something about the foreign contingent aboard this ship," he said.

"Foreign?" asked Jace. "Do you mean the—"

"The bearded men. You know who I mean. I don't know what they call themselves."

"The Lotacryllans," said Bryce.

"What do you mean we should 'do something'?" Jace asked. His black brows had drawn together in a look between suspicion and dislike.

"I mean," replied Calvaley between his teeth, "they're figuring out a plan of some kind. I believe they mean to take over the ship."

"And what makes you think that?" Jace's tone held a note of skepticism. "I've spoken with several of them, including the man who seems their unofficial leader, Rebane. They're always civil and polite, friendly, I could say. I haven't detected—"

"What would you know about it?" interjected Calvaley scornfully. "You aren't military. Have you ever even fired a weapon? How would you know what signs to look for?"

Jace seemed unsure what to say. He turned to Bryce for his opinion, but he also didn't know how to respond to Calvaley's allegation.

"What exactly have you seen?" he asked.

"Conversations that are shut down the moment I appear. Men lurking where they've no business to be. They're running recon on the ship, figuring out where everyone is and at what times. I know it."

Was it possible Calvaley was right? The evidence for his suspicions seemed weak. Was the old man going senile, perhaps as an effect of his prolonged time in Deep Sleep? He'd seen the state Calvaley had been in when he'd come out of stasis. He'd barely been alive, and Carina had said he had another collapse just after the medics discharged him.

Bryce felt sorry for him, but he wasn't at all sure he believed him.

"I would advise against antagonizing the Lotacryllans with accusations," said Jace. "We've only just regained their trust after their walkout over Pappu's incarceration."

Calvaley huffed in disgust.

"But if they *are* planning something...?" Bryce's gut tightened. The Black Dogs' and Lotacryllans' numbers were evenly matched. If Mezban's soldiers attempted a takeover and they had the advantage of surprise, they might just succeed.

On the other hand, if he put them in confinement based only an old man's delusions, that would be certain to piss them off. It might even incite the mutiny Calvaley suspected them of planning.

He didn't know what to do.

19

Vasya Rebane was an imposing figure. Like all the Lotacryllan men, he was tall, broad, and well-muscled, and he sat imperiously, his arms folded and knees spread wide.

Calvaley had taken a seat opposite him and was matching the man's frank stare with one of his own. The former Sherrerr admiral had decided to print himself a Black Dog uniform to wear to the meeting.

It had taken Bryce a moment to recognize the dark blue pants and sweater for what they were. The mercs generally slopped around in civilian clothes unless they were suited up for battle. It was one example of the changes that had taken place since Cadwallader and Atoi's deaths.

The line between the military and non-military contingents, the latter mostly made up by the mages, was becoming blurred. To Bryce, the change in attitude made sense. The Black Dogs were no longer being paid, they'd come along on the voyage to Earth by their own choice, and so they were not so much defenders of the mages but fellow adventurers. The two groups were blending to one, and that promised to be a good thing.

Except the same couldn't be said of the Lotacryllans.

Bryce hadn't paid particular attention until Calvaley voiced his suspicions, but when he thought about it, he realized the bearded men had been keeping themselves apart from the *Bathsheba's* other passengers. He really hadn't seen much of them at all. Perhaps he'd been remiss in not doing more to integrate the two sides, though Carina hadn't said anything about that before she left.

Jace certainly appeared to think so. After Calvaley had departed his cabin the previous evening, the mage had expressed his regret at what he thought was an oversight. *I've been too preoccupied with Nahla and mage matters,* he'd said. *I'm not sure I believe Calvaley's accusations are reliable, but I knew the Lotacryllans were feeling isolated and disenfranchised and have done little to address the problem. I've made a mistake. I'll do my best to correct it.*

So here they were. After listening to both Calvaley's and Jace's concerns, Bryce had invited Rebane to meet up and discuss 'ship's business'.

Bryce had also invited Jackson, the longest-serving Black Dog, to represent the mercs' interests. The man was resting his prosthetic arm on the table. Was he trying to match Rebane's subtly threatening attitude? It was hard to tell. Jackson's expression was mild and friendly, like Jace's, except Bryce doubted the merc's was genuine.

Jace poured mugs of cha and passed them out, introducing the drink in an amiable manner. Jackson lifted his mug and, after a tentative sniff, took a drink. He nodded and put his mug down. Neither Rebane nor Calvaley touched theirs, continuing their eye-to-eye standoff.

Bryce began to regret allowing Calvaley to attend.

He gave a small cough. "I thought it would be a good idea to discuss what happens aboard ship while Carina's party is away buying fuel."

"I'm here to discuss only one thing," said Rebane, his unblinking gaze not moving from Calvaley's eyes, "and that's the release of Pappu."

"I thought that had already been discussed," Bryce said.

"Not to my satisfaction," Rebane retorted. He thrust a finger at Calvaley. "*He* was released. Why not Pappu?"

"I believe Carina made some accommodations for the prisoner," said Jace. "He's allowed regular visitors and whatever material he chooses for entertainment."

"They are not enough." Rebane finally switching his attention away from Calvaley. His hardened features softened marginally as he spoke to the mage. "We appreciate your efforts on Pappu's behalf, but he isn't the type of person who can tolerate being confined alone for long periods. If his brother were still alive it would be different. Lomang was Pappu's guide in life. He looked up to his older brother and followed him in everything. Without him, and trapped in the brig, the man is going crazy. There's no telling what he might do—to himself."

Calvaley snorted derisively. "That wouldn't be any great loss. He's a thug and a murderer, from what I've heard."

Rebane's head snapped around to return his attention to the old man. "A thug and murderer?" he asked grimly. "Aren't we all thugs and murderers?"

Jackson studied the fingernails of his natural hand.

Jace cast his gaze upward for a beat and then said, "I think I can safely say I've never killed anyone. Not anyone human, anyway."

"The voyage isn't over yet," Jackson muttered.

"So you'll only be satisfied with Pappu's release?" asked Bryce.

"You read my mind," Rebane replied sarcastically.

"Absolutely not," said Calvaley.

Rebane shot to his feet, leaned menacingly over the table, and slammed down his hands in front of the old man before saying, "And who the hell are *you*?"

Calvaley pushed his head forward until his face was a centimeter from Rebane's. "More of a soldier than you'll *ever* be."

"Whoa," said Jace, also rising to his feet, and flapping his hands in a gesture of placation. "Nothing has been decided yet. We're here to talk, so let's talk, okay? Please," he said to Rebane, "sit down."

The Lotacryllan's features worked as if he were debating what to do, or perhaps struggling to overcome his anger. Calvaley's cold gaze still fixed on him, he lowered himself into his seat.

"Let's put aside the question of what happens with Pappu for a moment," Bryce said to Rebane. "I don't think your men's participation in our journey has ever been formally discussed. You joined us when we escaped the Regian planet, at our invitation—"

"Exactly," Jackson interjected.

"Since then, none of you has said you want to leave the ship, so we've assumed you're coming with us."

Rebane averted his gaze. "We cannot return to our home planet without Mezban."

Bryce guessed the Lotacryllans' loss of their commander must be shameful in their culture, whether her death was their fault or not. "Then, if you're staying with us, we need to find a way to get along. We don't want to spend the whole time at each other's throats."

Rebane grunted noncommittally.

"'Getting along', as you put it," said Calvaley, "is only one of several possible options."

"I don't think we have any alternative, do we?" Jace asked.

"We can't live in constant conflict and fear of our fellow passengers."

"There are most definitely alternatives," Calvaley countered, "though perhaps they're better discussed in private."

The Lotacryllan's eyes narrowed as he gazed at the old man. "This isn't private?"

"*No*," Calvaley replied emphatically.

Bryce wondered at his sudden apparently firm sense of allegiance to the Black Dogs. He was behaving as though he was a lifelong member, not Carina's former sworn enemy. Perhaps he felt he owed her a debt of gratitude for saving his life on Ostillon, or perhaps he felt siding with the mercs might help ensure his continuing survival. Whatever the answer was, Bryce wasn't sure whether Calvaley was a help or a hindrance in their cause. He seemed to be only making tensions with the Lotacryllan worse, but it was possible the show of resistance against Rebane's requests could deter them from rebelling.

"What if we organize some social events?" asked Jace. "A simple gathering in the twilight dome, for example. We can get to know each other a little better. Lotacryllans enjoy a drink, don't they, Vasya? And mercs are the same, it goes without saying. Am I right?" He looked from Rebane to Jackson. The Black Dog smirked, but Rebane's features remained antagonistic.

The mage seemed to deflate. "I'm not sure what else to suggest."

"I have a suggestion," said Rebane. "Release Pappu. That's all we ask. We don't want to cause problems. We want to live in harmony with our..." he paused as though trying to think of the right word, and his expression turned conciliatory "...our benefactors. We know you could have easily left us with the Regians. I cannot say with any certainty that, if our positions had been reversed, we would have done the same, and so that makes us especially grateful. But we cannot tolerate a poor, simple man's imprisonment. If you were to give him his freedom, relations between we Lotacryllans and the Black Dogs would improve. We would truly look upon them as our friends."

Calvaley turned to Bryce. "I strongly advise against this proposal."

"I think we should give it some consideration," said Jace, "as a gesture of reconciliation and friendship."

Bryce wasn't sure what to do. Pappu's confinement was clearly a big sticking point. Rebane was constantly pushing for his release. Had the Lotacryllans factored him into a plan to mutiny?

If Carina were here, he had no doubt she would not let Pappu out, but her stance was always combative and in the past that had sometimes worked against her.

Calvaley was of the same opinion, but he was another antagonistic personality. Jace obviously disagreed with the old man, yet he had no real military experience. He was concerned with smoothing the Lotacryllan's ruffled feathers.

On the side for releasing Pappu were Rebane and Jace. Calvaley was against it.

"Jackson," Bryce said, "what do you think? Should we let Pappu out of the brig?"

"Not in a fucking million years," the merc growled.

Two for, two against.

He had the deciding vote.

All gazes were upon him. He looked from Rebane, to Jackson, and at the two other men.

He rubbed the top of his head, trying to figure out what to do for the best. Finally, he said, "Okay, Pappu goes free, for now."

20

I t was the middle of the quiet shift when Ferne started shouting out in pain. Bryce had been deeply asleep, dreaming of Ithiya. He'd been a child again, in the mountains near his home, snow-gliding with his younger brothers and sisters. Except, in the dream, he'd fallen face first into a snow drift, and when he'd managed to extricate himself, his siblings were nowhere to be seen. His parents had disappeared, too. He'd called out, shouting their names, but only his own voice had replied, echoing back at him from the dark trees.

Ferne's yells blended with his own shouts in his mind as he wakened, the external noise dragging him up from the depths of his subconscious. He opened his eyes in darkness, the threads of his dream still clinging to his thoughts.

Disoriented, he lay still. Where was he? What was that—

Ferne!

He threw back his covers and leapt out of bed.

"Light! Door, open!"

The room burst into illumination.

Bryce ran for the door, reaching it before it fully opened. He turned sideways to slip through the gap.

Meanwhile, Oriana had also started hollering. "Ferne, what's wrong? Somebody help! Please help Ferne!"

As Bryce raced across the living area of the suite, Nahla's door opened. The little girl stood in the doorway, clutching an item of clothing to her chest, her long, dark brown hair a messy halo.

"What's...?" she asked, but Bryce didn't hear the rest.

He'd reached the twins' bedroom seconds after he awoke.

Ferne was sitting up in bed, holding his head, still yelling. Oriana leaned over him, her arm across his shoulders.

When Bryce appeared she looked up. Her eyes were shiny and her chin trembled. "Please help him, Bryce. I don't know what's wrong."

"Yeah, of course. I'll comm for a medic." He sent out the request, and then sat on the other side of Ferne from Oriana.

The boy was hunched over as if in great pain. Bryce had never seen anything like it. Was Ferne suffering from a brain disease? Surely it would be impossible to catch a disease on the ship. Or had something happened to Ferne on the Regian planet, and they were only seeing the effects now?

Bryce also held the boy and waited tensely for the medic to arrive.

Suddenly, Ferne's hands fell to his sides and he flopped backward onto his pillows. He was pale and sweat shone on his upper lip and forehead. He exhaled, letting out a moan of relief. "Ugh, that was terrible!"

"Is it over?" Oriana asked. "Are you feeling better? What was wrong with you?"

Ferne massaged his temples. "Yes, I think it's over. I think he finally shut up."

"Huh?" asked Oriana. "What are you talking about?"

Nahla walked into the bedroom, still holding onto the piece of clothing. "Is Ferne sick?"

"No, I'm not sick," he replied, though his tone remained strained.

The external door chime sounded, and Bryce told it to open. A Black Dog medic ran in, a bag of equipment in his hand. He came straight into the bedroom, paused, and looked around before focusing on Ferne.

"Is this the patient?"

"Yes," replied Bryce. "Something's wrong with his head. He was in a lot of pain."

"Nothing's wrong with my head," said Ferne irritably. "I'm fine now."

"Hmm," the medic said. "It won't hurt to take a look." He strode to the bed and deposited his bag on the cover. "Have you hit your head recently?" He opened the bag and pulled out a hand held scanner.

"No!" Ferne exclaimed. "If everyone would just be quiet a minute and let me speak I'll tell you what was wrong with me."

Everyone in the room paused and waited.

"Darius was Sending to me. Or, more like, he was *screaming* at me." Ferne looked at Oriana. "You know how powerful his Casts can be. He was excited."

Ferne shook his head and pulled himself upright.

"I'd still like to take a look at you," the medic persisted. "Brain injuries can be subtle, and they have wide-ranging effects that are harder to fix the longer they're left untreated."

"It'd be best to have a quick checkup," urged Bryce. "You know Carina would want you to."

After a sigh, Ferne said, "Go ahead. But there's nothing wrong with me."

Bryce moved out of the medic's way as the man walked to Ferne's side. He held the scanner to the side of the boy's head and waited until the machine beeped. Checking the screen, he nodded. "You'll be relieved to hear there *is* a brain in there."

He chuckled at his own joke while Ferne rolled his eyes.

"You're fine," the medic added, and began to walk back toward his bag.

"I *know*," Ferne said. "I just have an annoying younger brother."

"But reach out again if the pain returns," said the man. "It doesn't hurt to be cautious, and these things..." he waggled the scanner "...aren't infallible."

Oriana returned to her bed and pulled her covers over her knees while the man put away the scanner and closed his bag.

Ferne stuck the heels of his hands in his eyes and rubbed before saying, "Darius was telling me something really odd. I don't know whether to believe him."

"I'll get out of your way," said the medic.

He left, and Nahla said softly, "Can I sleep with you, Oriana?"

"Sure," Oriana replied, lifting a corner of her bedspread. "Hop in."

The little girl had clearly been unnerved by her abrupt awakening, and Ferne's yelling must have also been traumatic for her.

"What was Darius saying?" Bryce asked Ferne. "Are they all okay down on Magog?"

"It was a bit jumbled," Ferne replied, "but, basically, he kept repeating, *Mages. They're all mages, Ferne.*"

"Everyone on Magog is a mage?" Oriana asked in wonder.

"That's what it *sounded* like," said Ferne, "but I don't think that could be true, could it? He must be confused."

"Yeah," Oriana said. "He *is* only seven."

"If Darius says it, it has to be true," said Nahla petulantly.

The emotion was unusual for her, and when Bryce looked at her he saw the clothing she was holding onto was Darius's pajama top. He realized she must be missing her little brother more than he'd thought.

"It'll be cool if he's right," Ferne said. "A whole planet of mages? We wouldn't have to go to Earth. No need for years and years of Deep Sleep. We could live on Magog the rest of our lives."

Oriana's eyes widened as she appeared to consider the possibilities. "I would *love* to live in a cloud city. We could start our own design business, Ferne, selling clothes to mages. I bet they would buy our stuff. It's exactly what mages would like."

"Can you Send back to him and ask him to explain?" Bryce asked Ferne. "Or would his reply be too painful to receive?"

Ferne grimaced at the suggestion. "Even if his answer wasn't going to blow my head off, I can't Send that far. None of us can, only Darius. I tried replying when he was talking to me, telling him to quieten down, but he couldn't hear me. It was like a one way comm. I certainly hope he waits until he gets back before he tells me anything else he finds exciting."

A whole planet of mages!

Bryce mulled over the news. He guessed it could be possible. The mages had departed Earth in several ships, according to the documents they'd stored on Ostillon. A group of them might have settled in Geriel Sector and never been driven out or into hiding by the following waves of non-mage emigrants. The Lotacryllan man, Justus, hadn't mentioned anything about mages on Magog at the meeting, but they would be unlikely to tell outsiders about their powers.

If that was so, Oriana was correct: the discovery threw a whole new light on things. Carina had wanted to go to Earth because she hoped to find a safe place for mages to live. Magog could be that place, which meant they didn't need to go any farther. They could abandon their voyage right here.

There was only one way to be sure—comm Carina and ask her. But in order to do that he needed to go to the bridge to use the ship's external comm. The Black Dogs techs hadn't managed to integrate it with the internal system.

Bryce yawned. Ferne had already snuggled down into his bed, and Oriana was cuddling Nahla.

The suite was silent. Even the barely perceptible hum of the *Bathsheba's* drive was absent as the ship hung in space without fuel.

Mages on Magog?

Bryce decided the question could wait until morning.

21

The mansion among the clouds reminded Parthenia of her father's estate on Ithiya. Kai Wei had taken them on a tour as soon as they'd arrived. Though at the time she'd been so shocked by his announcement that he and many others on Magog were mages she hadn't been able to take in much of what she was seeing, now the memories of the rooms and areas she'd seen were returning to her in dribs and drabs.

She recalled the long, wide room with the high ceiling that Kai had said was the place he held his social receptions. Tasteful sofas, chaise longues, and straight-backed chairs dotted the edges of the space but the center was empty—for dancing and 'mingling', as Kai put it. She also remembered the formal garden, lamps lining the walkways and angled lights illuminating the decorative fountain displays. Under the starscape it had been breathtaking. The garden probably looked even more beautiful in daylight when all the many trees, hedges, plants, and flowers could be properly seen.

Kai had shown them the guest suites where they would be staying—the time restriction of their offplanet visitor statuses was erased, he reassured them. The beds had looked sumptuous, soft, and comfortable, and each suite contained its own food printer for guests to make snacks whenever they wanted.

Parthenia smiled. Ferne and Oriana would love *that* aspect of the bedrooms. What a shame they hadn't come on the trip. Nahla, too. But they would arrive soon, she was sure, and then they would be so excited.

Most amazing to her, and something very different from the home where she grew up, was Kai's work room. He'd taken them there last before their final stop in the informal lounge where she now sat.

She'd never seen a mage's workplace before, but when she saw his, everything about it made perfect sense. The most noticeable aspect of the place was the fact it was windowless. It was the only room in the house that had no windows, Kai had said, and it was soundproofed. The walls were solid blocks of deep, midnight blue, and the only furnishings were thick, square pillows made from rich brocade and two low tables: one held a jug of elixir and a cup and the other contained an embedded interface. An unseen atomizer filled the air with a spicy, woody scent.

Parthenia had thought it was the perfect space for Casting. No distracting external noises or sights, comfortable places to sit, and a pleasant aroma to help focus the mind. When she'd seen the room, she'd imagined herself in it, making important Casts in the government of Magog, as Kai did.

He was relaxing on a settee as he chatted about his duties, his back toward a window that looked out over the garden. Still coming to terms with the amazing revelation about the people of the planet, Parthenia was having problems focusing on what he was saying. Slim and tall, he looked elegant despite his casual posture. His mid-brown hair was cut very short, neatly grazing his ears, and he had a groomed beard like the Lotacryllan men, except his only encircled his mouth and extended a little way down his throat. He wore pants made from the hide of an animal and a pale green tunic made from a thick material.

Carina was sitting with Darius on a two-seater sofa side on from Kai, and Halliday and Justus sat opposite them. Kamil and Parthenia were together, facing the Magogian mage. Hsiao sat by herself in an armchair to Parthenia's right.

Her gaze drifted to the view behind Kai. Predawn light was already filtering into the sky, dimming the stars. The days and nights passed so quickly on Magog. She felt disoriented and muddled, partly due to the sudden change in their fortunes, she guessed, but also partly due to the fact that night was passing to day and she hadn't been to sleep. How did Magogians arrange their schedules? Did the government impose a rota?

"Parthenia," said Kai, leaning forward and putting his elbows on his knees. "It *is* Parthenia, right?"

Was he going to call her out for her lack of manners in not paying attention to him? Abashed, she replied, "Yes, that's right."

"Can I interest you in a pastry?"

On the table between the sofas and armchairs, dishes of sweet pastries had appeared. She'd been so immersed in her thoughts she hadn't even noticed anyone bringing them in.

"Oh, no, thank you," she replied. "I'm not hungry."

Darius was already munching on a flaky confection, crumbs showering down his front as he perched on the edge of the sofa, kicking his legs.

"If you're sure," said Kai with a smile.

He returned to his monologue—the man certainly loved to talk. "So, all in all, I'd say things run pretty smoothly. Mages do take a larger role in government than non-mages, but that's only to be expected. Our abilities make us very useful to have around, so, I have to admit, there is some bias toward us. However, we do our best to keep things equitable."

As he paused for breath, Justus managed to slip in a question: "What is it you do exactly?"

"I'm head of the Trade Office," Kai replied. "Imports and exports. That's why I'm based here. Japheth spaceport is the largest in Magog and it's where most offplanet imports arrive. The customs officers here really know their stuff." He gave a wink. "Exports tend to go out from all over the planet," he added, picking up a pastry.

"Can I interest anyone else?" he asked, holding it up. "They're delicious, and Darius and I can't eat them all by ourselves."

"Yes we can!" Darius declared, his words muffled by his full mouth.

Carina frowned at him, but then, before Kai could start up again she said, rather tersely, "You still haven't explained how you knew we had mages in our party."

Parthenia winced at her sister's almost-accusatory tone. She wasn't being very polite, considering Kai was treating them like honored guests.

He opened his mouth to answer, but Carina continued, "I guess it was from our saliva samples."

Kai closed his mouth and paused, perhaps allowing Carina time to go on. When she said nothing, he replied, "You're right. All the samples are screened, just in case." He took a bite of his pastry.

"In case of what?" Carina asked.

Kai chewed and swallowed. "In case we have any mage visitors," he replied amiably. "We don't advertise the fact that mages live on Magog. That decision to keep us a secret was taken a very long time ago, and no one's found any good reason to change it since. If it were to get out to the rest of the region that Magogians have undue...ahem...*influence* on business visitors, there could be serious repercussions. Other worlds might refuse to trade with us, or we mages could become a target to offworlders. They might want to kidnap us and force us to use our powers in their favor." He shrugged and took another bite of the dainty delicacy.

"Who knows what might happen?" he went on after a moment. "But those concerns shouldn't prevent us from welcoming fellow mages to our planet. We're very happy to have you, and we'd be even more pleased if you decided to stay."

Parthenia felt Kamil shift position as he perked up upon hearing Kai's last statement. Everything seemed to be fitting in with Kamil's plan for the two of them to abandon the voyage to Earth and live out the rest of their lives on Magog. Despite all the apparent advantages, she was unsure how she felt about the idea. Everything was happening too fast. She needed time to think.

"Wait a minute," Justus said. "What do you mean 'undue influence on business visitors'?"

"He means Enthralling them," Carina replied curtly. "It's a mind control Cast. The same one we used to make Poppy take us to the *Bathsheba* after we escaped the Regian planet."

"Dammit!" Justus exclaimed. "My dad fell victim to that. He said he couldn't understand why he always seemed to strike such bad deals on Magog. It wasn't until he was on his way home that he realized what he'd agreed to would barely bring him a profit."

Kai chuckled uncomfortably. "We follow a code of conduct that prohibits us from acting unethically. No trader leaves the planet worse off than when he arrived. It would be bad for business, after all."

"Yeah, but my dad wasn't much better off, either," said Justus testily.

Kai held up his hands. "I apologize. What else can I say?

Business dealings are a matter of each side pitting their negotiating skills against the other. I think I'm probably not wrong in saying your father made some very successful deals in his time, when he made a big profit at someone else's expense?"

Justus begrudgingly nodded.

"What we do isn't any more than using our skills to our advantage, the same as your father did. Only *we* have a code that means we never take things too far."

Parthenia wasn't entirely convinced by Kai's reasoning. Her father had forced her to Enthrall dealers and merchants at business meetings in order to make them agree to unfavorable terms with the Sherrerrs. At the time, she'd felt what she was doing was wrong, and she wasn't sure Kai was doing anything very different, despite his talk of a code of conduct.

Carina appeared unconvinced, too—by anything Kai had said, in fact. Through all his talking since they'd sat down she'd been wearing a sour look. But then, her sister's face often bore that same expression.

"We're getting very serious and dull," said Kai. He glanced over his shoulder to the view outside, and then said, "The sun will be up soon. What do you say we all go out to the terrace and watch the dawn? It looks like it'll be spectacular today. Then you can relax for a day or two, do your business deal, whatever it is you have in mind, and see a little more of Magog. Take your time, and think about whether you'd like to make our world your permanent home."

22

Carina was taking a solitary walk in Kai Wei's gardens. She'd comm'd Bryce and updated him on the situation on Magog. Her message would take hours to reach the *Bathsheba*, and there would be a similar delay before she received his reply. She didn't only want to let him know the surprising news that mages lived on the planet, she was also interested to hear what was happening aboard the ship.

She faced Wei's house, a hundred meters or so distant, but then changed her mind about returning there. The last few hours since arriving in Japheth had been rushed, chaotic, and astonishing. She needed time to think things through.

Turning away from the house and looking ahead, she saw a vista of clipped shrubs and tree canopies shaped like small clouds that was apparently endless, but the garden could not continue forever. Intrigued by what was causing the illusion, she set off with the intention of finding the boundary.

As Wei had predicted earlier, sunrise that day had been stunning. A field of rich red-gold had spread out across the horizon, taking up a third of the sky and edging high clouds with its color. But as swiftly as it had arrived, the dawn sky had shifted to blue, the clouds melted to nothing, and a new day had begun on Magog.

Now, the sun was already passing overhead. Carina had left her sunglasses at the house, but the trees overhanging the path provided protection from its brilliant beams. She followed the brick paths, checking that her back remained toward the house.

What a surprise Wei's greeting had been: *Welcome, fellow mages. Welcome to Magog.* She'd frozen with shock, and then she'd felt the urge to fight or run—her go-to reactions whenever she realized a stranger knew of her powers. But then she'd processed his words properly: *fellow* mages. The man had implied he was a mage, too.

Please don't be alarmed, he'd said, apparently in response to the look on her face. *You aren't in any danger.*

I'll be the judge of that, she'd thought, but everything that had happened since seemed to indicate Wei wasn't lying. He had no guards in his mansion. From what Carina had seen, he lived alone. Ronny, Malte, and Vasn had left when their host had invited them into his home. He also must have known the canisters she, Parthenia, and Darius carried at their sides contained elixir, yet he'd made no move to part them from the vital liquid.

She halted and looked behind her. The long, low buildings that comprised Kai Wei's home were obscured by vegetation. The air was growing hot, even under the overhanging branches. She unfastened the top buttons of her shirt before going on. The path she was following was straight and no other paths branched away from it as they had at the beginning of her walk.

How long had she been in the garden? Twenty minutes? Half an hour? Wei's estate was huge. He was clearly rich and influential. Everything she'd seen backed up his assertion that mages played an essential role in the government of Magog. And Wei himself was testament to the fact. His manner was not that of someone under another's control, a cowed slave playing a part. He was comfortable within his luxurious habitation and entirely at ease with being a gracious host.

A break in the line of hedges on her right revealed the side of a building, the first she'd seen since leaving the house. She stepped over the low shrubs at the path's edge and approached the edifice. Built of white blocks, the structure was room-sized and square at its base and narrowed as it rose to a point just above the treetops. She was reminded of the white buildings she'd seen in the distance from the spaceport.

Carina circled the building, trying to find the door, but there was none. The structure was solid all the way to the top.

She returned to the path and continued along it, thinking about Wei's suggestion that she and the other mages remain on Magog. She couldn't put her finger on the reason, but she felt uneasy at the prospect. Was it only that she was too fixed on the idea of voyaging to Earth on the *Bathsheba*? Or was it because, despite all that Wei told them and all she'd seen, she still found it all hard to believe.

Darius was definitely on board with living in a mansion and eating pastries all day, and Kamil seemed enthusiastic about the idea of settling on Magog, too. But Parthenia was, as always, keeping her feelings private. Carina had often thought her sister learned the habit as she was growing up, witnessing Ma's abuse but unable to show her disapproval out of fear of angering her father even more.

Justus was grumpy about Wei's admission that Magog's government employed mages to unfairly sway business negotiations in its favor. Hsiao was simply intrigued by the concept of living in the air, and Halliday was his usual taciturn merc self.

Carina was growing hotter. Surely she would reach the garden's boundary soon?

The path swerved to the left, and as she ambled down it, she saw Wei's mansion come slowly into view in the distance.

Huh?

She stopped.

At some point in her stroll she'd turned in the opposite direction.

She was annoyed. She only wanted to find the edge of the garden. Was that too much to ask?

Returning the way she'd come, rather than sticking to the path, this time she stepped off it and into the undergrowth.

The plants and shrubs in that area grew fairly wild and untamed, in contrast to the more controlled vegetation nearer the house. The shade was heavy and the air warm and moist. Carina soon found herself sweating as she pushed through the close-growing branches and thickly clustered leaves.

After a few minutes' effort, she came across a line of bare soil running directly across her path. About a meter across, the line looked as though it had been artificially created, perhaps by someone spraying a herbicide. Not a blade or grass nor weed stalk marred its emptiness. On the other side, the shrubs and trees continued, the same as in the place she was standing.

Noticing something odd about the vegetation she was facing, Carina studied it. Then she looked at the trees and shrubs directly above and around her.

They were the same!

The scene across the line of soil was a mirror image.

Instantly, her mind flew back to another time she'd seen a facsimile of a natural scene.

She stepped over the line of soil and reached out. At the point where the vegetation began again her arm disappeared. The trees, shrubs, undergrowth, even the scanty grass struggling to grow in the shade and dryness, all of it was an illusion.

Carina took another step, tentatively feeling ahead with her toes. She passed through the false scene and found herself standing in front of a high fence of thick mesh. The material was too thick to see through it. Above, the sky was clear blue and the sun eye-piercingly bright. Behind her was the image of the garden.

She'd found the garden boundary. What was more, the invisible barrier she'd passed through was the same as the illusion at the entrance to the Dirksens' mountain castle on Ostillon, created by mages in ancient times.

If she'd ever doubted that Kai Wei was a mage and her kind held a position of importance on Magog, she could safely cast aside that doubt now.

"I'm impressed," said a voice out of nowhere.

Carina jumped and spun around, looking for its owner.

Wei strode through the illusory field.

"In all my years living here," he went on, "I don't think anyone's ever made it to the end of my garden. How did you know how to get here?" He was relaxed and cheerful as usual, his expression open and friendly.

Yet Carina felt she'd done something she wasn't supposed to.

"I'm impressed, too," she countered, "by how well you hide the boundary, and the fact that as soon as I stepped through the fake image of the garden you knew what I'd done and exactly where I was."

"The Semblance is set with an alarm, which you triggered when you walked through it. I installed the alarm because it's dangerous on this side of the barrier. I wouldn't want anyone to fall to their deaths."

"So the edge of your estate is on the other side of this fence?"

To answer her, Wei lifted his arm and waved it across the mesh. The thick material disappeared, and suddenly Carina was looking out over the surface of Magog, thousands of meters below. The verdant jungle trees were so small they looked like weed floating on a pond.

She gasped. She was standing less than half a meter from a long fall and a sudden, deadly, stop.

"Don't worry," said Wei. He touched the place where the fence had been, and his hand met invisible resistance. "You would only be in danger if you climbed over the fence."

He waved again and the fence reappeared.

"You did that without drinking elixir," said Carina.

"It operates via technology. I didn't Cast to make it turn transparent or return it to its opaque setting. The fence responded to my gesture, that's all."

"And this?" Carina reached out toward the garden and her arm disappeared up to her shoulder. "You called it a 'Semblance'?"

"Yes, that *is* a Cast," Wei replied. "A permanent one, until another mage undoes it, that is. I think you knew that, though. You knew it wasn't real and you could pass through it."

"I saw something similar once before. I guessed mages had probably created it, but I was never certain until now."

"You've seen another Semblance? Fascinating," said Wei. "You must tell me all about it. Would you like to come back to the house? You must be tired of wandering around outside."

"Uh..." Carina was still curious about what else she might discover in the garden, but she was also interested to learn about the Semblance Cast. Wei might also know others Nai Nai had never taught her. "Sure."

The mage smiled, produced a small bottle from a pocket, opened it, and took a drink.

A second later, Carina was back inside the mansion, in the Casting room.

23

I'm not sure I trust Kai Wei. Something seems off about him, but I don't know exactly what. He's been a great host, very friendly and welcoming, except he tends to talk too much and that gets boring after a while. But his home is huge and beautiful and he's said we can stay here as long as we like, which is a big relief. The border control official at the spaceport only gave us eighteen hours. How could I have found a vendor and bought the fuel we need in eighteen hours?

Anyway, that problem's solved now. We have all the time we want to make the transaction, according to Wei. The bigger question is, do we even need the fuel? It's been made very clear that the Magog government would be happy to accommodate us if we decided to settle on their planet, and I think the offer also applies to whoever accompanies us, mage or not.

It's a generous proposal and I have to admit I'm tempted. Our voyage already nearly ended in complete disaster, and who knows what else is awaiting us out there? We might encounter more hostile aliens like the Regians, or fly into a spacetime anomaly. On the other hand, I've had my heart set on going to Earth for a long time. If I don't make it there, I might regret it for the rest of my life.

What do **you** *think about cutting our journey short and staying here? Magog seems to be a nice place, or this cloud city does, at least. I haven't been to the surface yet. It's very hot and humid down there, by all accounts. I don't think there are any military tensions in this part of the Geriel Sector, and there don't seem to be ruling clans like the Sherrerrs and Dirksens, so it's pretty safe.*

Let me know what you think. I miss you, and the kids. I hope things are okay aboard the ship. Comm me back as soon as you can. It'll be tomorrow in Magog before I hear from you!

Love you.

The tone that signaled the end of the comm played.

Bryce was on the bridge, and he'd been about to compose his own comm to transmit when Carina's arrived.

So it was true. Mages did live on Magog, and, not only that, one of them had invited Carina and her family to live there, too. From what she said, it sounded like Darius hadn't told her he'd already Sent the latest news to Ferne.

He wasn't sure what to make of it all. On the face of it, the new information was amazing. No one had imagined they might encounter mages before they even reached Earth, and, not only mages, but also a world where they lived free of the fear of persecution—the sanctuary Carina had hoped for.

Yet she seemed to have reservations, especially regarding this mage who had befriended them. Bryce wasn't surprised. Carina was cautious and distrustful to an extreme. It had taken him a long time to convince her he didn't mean her any harm, so he wasn't at all surprised she suspected Kai Wei's motives.

But the whole setup did seem too good to be true. Perhaps she was right to be skeptical. He hoped she and the rest of her party weren't in any danger.

In the middle of Bryce's musings, the bridge door opened and a large figure strode in.

When he saw who it was, Bryce tensed up. He hadn't seen Pappu in a while, not since the giant had helped his brother rouse all the Black Dogs from stasis, and he hadn't anticipated seeing him so soon after his release. The man must have come straight to the bridge after the guards had told him he was free to go.

Pappu marched quickly to where Bryce was sitting and thrust out his hand.

Bryce flinched and ducked, expecting a blow.

Then he saw the man was waiting expectantly, his arm extended.

Pappu wanted to shake hands.

"Thank you for giving the order to set me free," Pappu said in his usual low, rumbling tone.

Bryce straightened up in his seat, embarrassed to have made a fool of himself by assuming the giant was going to attack him, and grateful that no one else was on the bridge to witness it. Pappu didn't seem to have noticed his mistake.

Grasping the man's massive paw, Bryce said, "You're welcome. I'm sorry about what happened to your brother and sister-in-law."

Pappu's mouth turned down at the corners and for a few seconds he didn't respond. "Lomang was always good to me. If anyone had killed him, I would have avenged his death, but he was not murdered. A strange accident took him and Mezban and some soldiers. I saw them vanish with my own eyes."

"Yes," replied Bryce. "We're still not sure exactly what happened, except that it was something to do with a cloud of anomalous spacetime straying into our path."

Pappu looked perplexed.

"It was a terrible accident," said Bryce. "One we hope to avoid repeating."

"I wondered if it was the enchantress who did it, the same way she killed the woman prisoner. Lomang told me she had moved the woman out of the ship and into space to execute her.

But when my brother died, I saw the mercenaries disappear, too. I didn't think the enchantress would kill her own soldiers."

"No," said Bryce, realizing the 'woman prisoner' had been Sable Dirksen. "Definitely not."

Simply the possibility that Lomang could have died at Carina's hands had kindled a fire in the huge man's eyes that sent a tingle of fear through Bryce. "Definitely not," he repeated, and then, "Have you found a cabin? Most of the Lotacryllans are on the third deck."

Pappu nodded, but he seemed uninterested in Bryce's change of subject. "The enchantress has gone to buy fuel for the ship, hasn't she?"

"Yes, that's right. She's taken a few people with her, including a Lotacryllan man, Viggo Justus. She should be back in a few days."

"I think, if she was here, I would not have been allowed to leave the brig. She would have forbidden it."

"That's most likely true," said Bryce. "Carina's very cautious, especially when it comes to keeping her family safe. And you and she have some history. You aren't her favorite person by a long shot."

His expression grave, Pappu nodded again. "She was a formidable enemy. No one else has ever managed to restrain me, even if she did need the help of a mech to do it." He smiled wryly. "I hope now she will be a formidable ally."

He turned as if to leave, but then halted and turned back to Bryce. "Do you not find her frightening? She can enslave your mind and make you tell her all your secrets."

"Yes, well, she only does that to her enemies, and only if she absolutely has to."

"Hmm. I'm not sure you're right about that."

Without another word, Pappu clumped out of the bridge.

As the door closed, Bryce relaxed. Though the giant had

wanted to be friendly, there was something about him that put Bryce on edge—probably the man's sheer size.

Or was it that he already had reservations about releasing him? He didn't think the giant posed a great risk. He might be big, but brawn didn't count for much against a pulse rifle, and he wasn't capable of organizing a mutiny.

What really had Bryce worried was Carina. When she found out Pappu had been released, she was going to be *mad*.

AFTER RECORDING and transmitting his message, Bryce left the bridge and took the elevator to the top level of the ship, and then headed down the passage toward Jace's cabin. The mage would be very interested to hear the away party had discovered mages lived on Magog.

When he reached the right door, he knocked, expecting that the chime remained inactivated.

There was no answer.

Once more, he rapped the door with his knuckles.

When Jace still didn't open it, he tried the comm system. Jace sometimes wore an ear comm, though not reliably.

Jace's comm was turned off.

Is he asleep?

It wasn't the quiet shift, but it would be easy for the mage's daily routine to get out of whack.

Perhaps he's only meditating.

Bryce hesitated.

He could be somewhere else on the ship.

Bryce thought up a few more reasons why Jace wasn't answering his door.

Then he knocked again.

Seconds of silence passed.

He spoke to the ship's computer. Before Carina had left for Magog, she'd added him, Jace, and Jackson to the list of people with authority to override the *Bathsheba's* security systems.

In response to his request, the door to the cabin unlocked and opened.

24

Jace's room was a mess. The low table had been knocked over, a jug lay on its side, and cha or elixir had splashed across the floor. The bedclothes were strewn about, and one of the chairs had been upended. It was obvious some kind of struggle had gone on.

Bryce ran to the bathroom and looked inside. It was neat and tidy. The fight hadn't spread in here, but, like the main room, it was empty, with no sign of Jace.

Someone had forced their way into his room and taken him. Probably more than one person. Though he was a pacifist, the mage was a large and powerful man and he would not have been subdued easily.

The attack must have been fast, too. All he would have needed was one sip of elixir to Send to Oriana or Ferne that he needed help.

"*Damn*," Bryce muttered as he gazed at the disruption.

Returning to the outer door, he looked into the passageway. As usual in that part of the ship, no one was around.

He comm'd Jackson and told the merc what he'd seen.

"Fuck," was Jackson's response. "The Lotacryllans didn't waste any time, did they?"

"No. It has to be them who've taken him. I can't see any blood, so I'm hoping he isn't badly hurt."

"It's early days yet," Jackson said bitterly. "After all we did for them. Ungrateful bastards."

"I expect we'll hear from them any minute," Bryce said. "I spoke to Pappu just a short while ago, on the bridge. He came to thank me for releasing him. He seemed to be genuine, but now I think he was only keeping me distracted while they captured Jace."

"Sounds like it. Lucky it wasn't you they took."

"The area around the bridge is too busy. Too many mercs wandering around. The armories are all secure, right?"

"Yeah," Jackson replied. "What gets me is, they're so dumb. The *Bathsheba's* going nowhere until she has some fuel in her, and Carina isn't going to fill her up while the Lotacryllans are holding Jace hostage."

"They probably think it's gonna be easier to take the ship while she isn't around," said Bryce, "and they're betting she'll give them the fuel to get Jace back."

The merc didn't reply.

"Jackson?"

Bryce waited.

"Jackson!"

When he finally replied, Jackson's voice jarred rhythmically and Bryce could faintly hear the man's running footsteps. "It's kicking off. There's fighting on Deck Three. The Lotacryllans have snatched Calvaley, too."

"Shit. He didn't do himself any favors at that meeting with Rebane. They think he's a danger, even though he's old."

"They aren't as dumb as I thought," Jackson said. "Calvaley has decades of military experience. They don't want him on our side." The merc gave an *Ooof!* as he encountered some hard physical contact.

"Gotta go," he said, and then his comm went dead.

Bryce comm'd Oriana.

"Hey, Bryce!" she answered.

"Hey. You, Ferne, and Nahla are in your suite, right?"

"Yes, we're—"

"Good. Cast Lock on the door. Keep Casting Lock. Don't go out, and don't open the door for anyone except me."

"But—"

"Do it, okay? I don't have time to explain why."

"Okay," she replied quietly. "Are we being attacked?"

"Yes, from within," Bryce replied before closing the comm.

He set off along the passageway.

He didn't think he'd ever been as grateful for the twins' mage powers as he was at that moment. They were only young, but they had the ability to protect themselves, and they'd been in several battles. They would do whatever was required to stay safe. Even if the Lotacryllans did manage to get into their suite, Oriana and Ferne could Transport out of there, taking Nahla with them.

He took the elevator down to Deck Three.

But when it arrived, the outer doors wouldn't open. The Lotacryllans had done something to jam them.

Muffled yells and the faint sounds of impacts came from outside.

He told the elevator to take him up a deck.

On Deck Four, the doors opened on the sight of Black Dogs running past.

Bryce sped out and followed them.

Up ahead, fighting men and women were clustered around one of the service access panels. Jackson was among them, tussling with a Lotacryllan man. Pappu was there, too, towering over everyone.

The service panel was open. Bryce realized the Lotacryllans were trying to get into it, and the Black Dogs were trying to stop them.

The enemy soldiers must have closed off the elevator doors before all their men had retreated to their deck, and now the mercs were trying to prevent them from making it there, perhaps with a view to taking a few hostages of their own.

He dove into the melee and grabbed the first Lotacryllan he saw. The man kicked out, driving his boot into Bryce's stomach.

All the air left him in one great, *whoof!* He collapsed among the flailing arms and legs, covering his head against any more blows. Someone tripped over him, landing in front of him. He recognized Rosa, the woman who had disarmed the bomb Mezban had planted in the twilight dome. Her right eye was swollen shut and blood dribbled from her busted upper lip.

Dragging air into his lungs, he forced himself to his feet.

In the few seconds that had passed while he'd been incapacitated, more Lotacryllans had made it to the access hatch. Black Dogs were attacking them on all sides, but the bearded men were fighting like wild animals—headbutting, kicking, attempting to gouge out eyes and land throat-punches, stomping mercs who were already down.

Pappu was causing a lot of damage and preventing the mercs from getting anywhere near the opening while his countrymen disappeared into it.

As Bryce watched, another Lotacryllan made it to the hatch.

The mercs were breaking upon the giant like waves against a rock. He seemed impervious to blows, and anyone who got too close was lifted up and thrown aside.

Bryce pushed forward. He reached out, trying to get at Pappu.

The big man saw his efforts and smiled.

Suddenly, all the Lotacryllans except Pappu were gone.

"Get down!" a voice yelled from somewhere behind.

Bryce ducked and turned.

A Black Dog called Gulay was racing over, carrying a pulse rifle. He was aiming at Pappu.

As the mercs ceased their assault to give Gulay a clear shot, the giant took his chance. Bryce turned back just in time to see him folding his bulk into the open hatch.

A pulse round hit his back.

The giant's shirt smoldered.

Pappu twitched, and then relaxed.

His weight carried him the rest of the way into the service tunnel, and he slipped from sight.

25

Kai Wei had insisted upon taking Carina and the others for a flight in his glider. The aircraft was stored in a hangar at the far side of his property, and they had to walk through a tunnel to reach it.

"After you," the mage said with a grin as he opened the entrance to the tunnel, which ran under the garden.

Carina walked down the steps, wondering if she'd made the right decision in agreeing to the trip.

Another night had passed on Magog, and no one had slept. They'd passed the time eating a lavish dinner and chatting. Wei had probed a little about the mages' histories, but each time he asked a prying question, Carina had steered the conversation away. She'd been pleased that Parthenia had been equally circumspect. Darius had been too busy eating to take much notice of anything. Wei hadn't been interested in the back-grounds of any of his other guests.

Carina was reluctant to go on Wei's offered tour of that region of Magog by air because she hadn't made any moves to buy fuel for the *Bathsheba* yet. The tour was only going to be another delay before she could complete the transaction she'd come there to make.

But what if they decided to settle on Magog? They wouldn't need any starship fuel, and the ember gems could be used to buy other things they would need.

She reached the bottom of the steps. Motion-activated lights blinked on, illuminating a chilly underground avenue, its floor and walls made from bricks.

Wei had passed her and was already walking ahead. "This way," he called out over his shoulder, and beckoned them. "It isn't far. About ten minutes' walk. It's faster this way. Avoids all those twisty garden paths. And drier if the weather's wet."

"Does it rain much up here?" asked Halliday.

"Quite a bit," Wei replied. "More than is strictly necessary. Often precipitation layers are so low we can raise the city above them, you see. But if we did that too much the gardens would get rather dry and brown and not at all pretty. So we tolerate rain showers now and then."

"What about storms?" Hsiao asked.

"This area sees very few storms. That's one of the reasons it was chosen as a cloud city site. When we *do* have them, they're spectacular!" Wei's eyes flashed in delight. "No rain or storms are forecast for today, however."

As they walked down the tunnel, Darius skipped ahead, while Parthenia and Kamil trailed behind, deep in whispered conversation. The couple had been doing that a lot since arriving on Magog, and Carina was beginning to wonder what it was they were always talking about. They didn't seem to be speaking secretively because they were excited to be in love. If anything, they seemed to be almost arguing.

Hsiao was grilling Wei about his glider even before she set eyes on it, and Halliday was striding along on his own. He'd grown quieter and quieter as Magog's lightning-fast days had passed.

Justus was walking alongside Carina.

"I don't imagine, when you signed up to work for Mezban," she said, "you ever thought you would end up on Magog, where your father once traded."

"Definitely not. We were told we would embark on an expedition out of Geriel Sector. That was what attracted me to the job. I was interested to see what people are like in other parts of the galaxy."

"And what did you find?"

He smiled. "That wherever you go, people are much the same."

"Ha," said Carina. "I guess that's right. You meet good and bad people all over. What's Lotacrylla like?"

Justus frowned before answering, "My world is a complicated place. Our nations have many layers, from Lomang and Mezban's class at the top right down to the poorest sectors, like ember gem miners."

"Ember gem miners are from the lowest classes?" Carina asked. Her hand instinctively moved to the pocket in her pants that held the jewels. She always kept them on her person.

"Yes," replied Justus. "It's a terrible job. Very dangerous and poorly paid. Only those who have no standing, no money, and no family or friends to support them do it."

"But ember gems are so valuable. How come the miners are poorly paid?"

"The mining companies pay subsistence wages and a commission for any gems found, but the chance of finding a gem is so low, most miners go their whole lives without receiving a commission payment. And because their wages are barely enough to pay for food, they can never save to make any change in their lives or investment in their future. Ember gem miners usually work until they die from ill health or accident, and then their bodies are placed in an exhausted, closed-off seam of the mine and forgotten."

"Shit," Carina said. "That's awful." She touched the pouch of gems in her pocket, fingering the hard nodules through the material. Then she withdrew her hand, feeling tainted and disgusted.

"It is what it is. Every so often a philanthropist calls for the regulations to be changed, but then the mining companies hold up one or two examples of miners whose lives were transformed when they found a gem. There's a little debate, and everything goes back to normal."

"I had no idea," said Carina. She felt somehow culpable for the fates of all the people who had suffered and died to find the gems she was carrying.

"Here we are," announced Wei.

He'd halted at the opening to stairs leading upward.

They climbed up them to the hangar.

Wei's glider was beautiful. The air vehicle stood alone in the storage space like a giant white bird preparing to lift into flight. The wings flared out gracefully from a slim body, and the nose tapered to a gentle point.

Hsiao appeared to fall in love at first sight. She walked to it and ran a hand across its hull. Then she spun around to face Wei, an imploring look on her face. "You have to let me fly her. You're going to let me, right?"

Like a father indulging a spoiled child, the mage replied, "But of course. Why else do you think I brought you here?"

He opened the door by voice command and steps descended.

Inside, the glider held rows of wide, luxuriously padded seats. Next to each pair of seats was a large window. Carina took a seat near the front while Hsiao joined Wei in the cockpit. Darius sat across the aisle from Carina, and Parthenia and Kamil sat behind her.

"Fasten your seat belts," Wei called out.

The glider was facing the hangar doors. They opened,

revealing the brilliant green expanse of the planet surface and a cloudless blue sky. The glider trundled slowly forward, ungainly in its movement.

It reached the edge of the hangar.

"Ready, everyone?" asked Wei.

Without waiting for a reply, he continued to pilot the glider onward.

A sloping runway protruded from the hangar, like a tongue poking out from a mouth. The glider's nose tipped down, following the slope.

"Oooooh!" Darius squealed.

The air vehicle was fast gaining speed. In another moment, it ran out of runway.

But they didn't fly off into the air.

They fell.

The glider had slipped off the runway and quickly moved from its forty-five degree angle to ninety degrees. It was plummeting to the ground.

Darius yelled.

Parthenia screamed.

Hsiao and Wei were arguing, but Carina couldn't make out the words. The wind that roared past them was too loud. All she could see was the jungle canopy racing up at a terrifying speed.

Hsiao hollered something, reached over and grabbed the controls. Suddenly, the glider's nose began to lift.

Within about the same, short amount of time they'd fallen, the air vehicle was flying parallel to the ground. The world had righted itself. In front of them, the horizon bisected the view, green below and blue above.

Wei was laughing.

26

That evening, at dinner, the atmosphere in Kai Wei's mansion had entirely changed. Darius was the only one who appeared oblivious to the events of the day. Carina was no longer in the mood for pleasant conversation, and the others in her party apparently felt the same way. They ate quietly, Wei's attempts to draw them out falling on deaf ears.

Through the stunned silence in the passenger cabin after the glider had pulled out of its dive, Wei had explained that the glider was equipped with a-grav. They'd never been in any danger, he'd said. He could have pulled up at any time, and he'd only wanted to inject a little fun into their excursion.

After his 'joke', he'd taken them on the tour of Magog that he'd promised. They'd flown over the jungle to the ocean, and then across the ocean to an archipelago, where they'd landed.

In another time and another place, Carina would have loved the little set of pristine islands set in a shallow, azure sea. They'd swum out to the reefs that encircled the archipelago and, with the help of borrowed equipment, they'd seen the beautiful corals and astonishing, colorful fish and other sea life.

Their next stop, as the sun was dropping quickly from the sky, was a larger, single island. They didn't land there, but flew in slow circles above it. As the sun disappeared and the stars came out, the reason Wei had taken them there became apparent. All around the shoreline the sea turned phosphorescent, glowing and shimmering as the waves swept in and out. Not long after that, luminous sea creatures became visible in the depths. The organisms' long bodies trailed out, threads of pulsating color.

The display had continued after Wei turned the glider for home, and Carina had stared out of her window at it until it was lost in the darkness.

In other circumstances, it would have been a wonderful day, and she would have seriously considered settling on Magog just to be able to return to those islands again and again.

But Wei's actions at the beginning of the day had thrown a pall over everything.

Despite all the hospitality he'd shown them otherwise, Carina's gut feeling about the man had been confirmed. He was not to be trusted. Whether he was only reckless and foolish, or whether, deep beneath his urbane exterior, he was malicious, she didn't know. However, she did know how to find out.

As the servitors brought in the dessert, Wei announced that it would probably be best if everyone retired to their rooms after dinner.

"I know it's hard for offworlders to keep track of time in their first few weeks here, but you've been awake three days and two nights now. You must be feeling tired."

"I certainly am," said Carina, and she meant it, but she was also looking forward to getting away from Wei for a few hours. "Darius, you're sleeping in my room, right?"

Her brother was about to cram a piece of cake in his mouth. He paused and replied, "Uh huh. I'd like that, Carina."

No one else was interested in the dessert. Wei had provided

a feast of meats, roast vegetables, fish, soup, salads, fried beans, flat breads, and sauces. All local produce, and all delicious. Despite her misgivings over Wei and his sense of humor, Carina had eaten more of his food than she needed.

"Do you have servants to prepare all this food?" Parthenia asked.

"No need," Wei replied. "Everything on the estate is automated. I prefer it that way."

Carina had wondered about that, too. It seemed odd that the entire place could run without human labor.

"I think I'll go to bed now," she said. "Come on, Darius."

"But I haven't finished..." He saw the look in Carina's eye, sighed, and said, "Okay."

As Carina stood up, he jumped down from his seat and ran to her side.

"Good night, everyone," she said.

"Are you sure you can remember where your room is?" asked Wei.

"Yes, I'm sure, thanks."

Holding Darius's hand, she left the dining room, relieved to finally get away from the mage. Her brother trotted alongside her.

"I think I ate too much," he said.

"I think you did, too," she replied. Then she looked down at him, smiling, and added, "And so did I. Mr. Wei's food is good, isn't it?"

"Yes. It tastes different from the food we eat on the ship."

"That's because it's fresh. On the *Bathsheba* the food's either been in storage or printed. It isn't the same as something fresh from a farm."

"Can we take some back with us?" asked Darius.

"Sure. After we buy the fuel, we'll go shopping for supplies. Is there anything you'd particularly like?"

Darius rattled off a list of foods, mostly sweet and unhealthy.

Carina was interested that he hadn't mentioned anything about staying on Magog and not returning to the ship. Though he was young, he had to have heard Wei's frequent mentions of the possibility. And he was clearly having a great time. Yet he wasn't putting up any fuss about leaving the planet.

She waited until they were in their guest suite before asking him anything on the matter, and even when the door was closed and they were behind solid walls, she wanted to keep her voice low, just in case spying devices were watching and listening to them.

She sat on the bed, sinking into the soft mattress, and said, "Can you come here a minute, Darius?"

The little boy had run to the mirror and was making faces at himself, but he immediately walked over to her.

"I want to play a whispering game," Carina said.

"Cool!" said Darius. "I'll go first."

"Okay."

He leaned in and said softly in her ear, "I think I'm gonna be sick."

Carina whispered back, somewhat alarmed, "Can you hold off being sick just a minute until after you answer a question?"

Darius considered a moment, and then nodded.

Gently holding his shoulders, she put her mouth so close to his ear her lips brushed it. "Darius, what kind of feeling do you get from Kai Wei? Is he a good or a bad person?"

She moved her head back and got a look at Darius's face, which had become very serious. He slowly shook his head.

That was all the answer Carina needed. She was naturally distrustful of everyone she met. Suspicion and wariness had been bred into her. But Darius was still young. He hadn't learned to always be skeptical of others' motives.

He put his cheek against hers and said quietly, "It doesn't

hurt too bad because you and the others are here with me, and you're all strong and good, but Mr. Wei feels like Castiel did. He's like a big, dark, shadow, full of hate."

Carina looked into her brother's eyes. He stared back at her with candor, appearing older than his seven years.

Wei is a Dark Mage?

If Darius's impression was accurate—and Carina had no reason to doubt it—they were all in dire danger. Castiel had been vicious and ruthless, willing to enslave, betray, and torture his own family to get what he wanted, and he'd only been a teenager.

Wei was a grown man, experienced in manipulating people. He'd led them to believe he was a generous host, sometimes a bore, but otherwise a kind man, though Carina had thought his 'catching' her when she crossed his garden's boundary rather strange. Then, today, the mask had properly slipped, and, unable to control himself, he'd given into his desire to fill them with fear, to have them under his control.

How much of all that he'd told them was true? In the brief time they'd spent in Japheth, the Magogian behavior they'd seen hadn't given Carina any reason to think they were mages. The people here seemed very different from the mages she'd met at the Matching in Pirine, who were peaceful people, content with simple things and pleasures.

Was Wei hiding his powers from the government? Was that why he lived in seclusion? He appeared to have some kind of relationship with the officers of the Mayor's Watch who had brought them there, but he could have Enthralled them.

Darius was watching her.

"Thanks for telling me about Wei," she said. "It's time to get ready for bed now."

"Are we really staying here tonight?" he asked.

Carina raised her eyebrows. "You know what? Sometimes I think you don't only read my feelings, you read my mind."

He shrugged.

Perhaps Darius could hear her thoughts, or perhaps it was only common sense to know they must leave, and soon. Wei was probably already contemplating the repercussions of his unwise prank and wondering if he should make a move to ensnare the offworld mages quickly, before they left the sphere of his control. Each minute they spent under the Dark Mage's roof brought them closer to danger.

"Maybe not the whole night," she said. "Do you still feel sick?"

He shook his head.

"Good. You need to get some sleep. I'll wake you when I decide what to do."

27

"I can't believe you still want us to live here after what happened today," said Parthenia.

"And *I* can't believe you would let one stupid joke prejudice you against an entire planet," retorted Kamil in a fierce whisper.

They were standing in the corridor outside their guest rooms. Kai had given them separate suites next door to each other.

Parthenia hadn't wanted to discuss the subject of her and Kamil settling on Magog yet again, especially not when she was overfull, tired, and out of sorts. But he'd brought it up when they'd arrived at their rooms, and within a few minutes their conversation had devolved into an argument.

He hadn't stopped talking about his idea the whole time they'd been at Kai's estate, alternating between subtle and not-so-subtle attempts to pressure her into agreeing. It was like he was obsessed with the idea and couldn't leave it alone.

At some point, Parthenia had suddenly understood why Kamil had joined the military when he was only sixteen. He must have gotten infatuated with that idea, too, and left behind his life and family on his home world based on a whim that had grown into a compulsion.

She wasn't even sure any longer if she didn't want to settle on Magog, or if she was just sick and tired of him trying to force her into it.

"Let's talk about it tomorrow, Kamil," she said. "I'm exhausted."

As he went to reply, his features were full of irritation, but then his facial expression relaxed and he looked a little shameful. "You're right. We can discuss it again tomorrow. It's just I think this would be a great place to live, for *both* of us."

Parthenia stiffened.

"Sorry, sorry," said Kamil, holding up his hands. "We can talk in the morning."

He grasped her waist and pulled her close to kiss her.

She didn't resist. She *did* like him, a lot—when he wasn't obsessing about living on Magog.

They parted.

"Good night," said Parthenia.

"Good night," Kamil replied. "Hey, I wonder if it'll be daylight or night when we wake up?"

"I don't know. I'm too tired to think about it." She walked the few steps to the door of her suite. "Sleep well."

After going inside and closing the door, relief swept over her. Between Kamil's incessant pressure and the busy schedule of socializing Wei had imposed on them, she didn't think she'd had a minute to herself. But now she had time alone, she didn't want to do anything except sleep.

In a daze of sleepiness, she took a shower and got ready for bed. Yellow, silken pajamas in her size lay on the bedspread. She put them on, climbed onto the high bed, and slipped under the covers. The last thing she remembered was her head touching the pillow.

"Parthenia."

She recognized Carina's voice instantly, but what was her sister doing in her room?

Parthenia opened her eyes onto darkness, a shadowy form above her.

"What are you *doing*?" she asked crossly. How long had she been asleep? She still felt tired. She squinted at Carina through sore, itchy eyes.

"Get up," Carina said softly but urgently. "We have to leave."

"Huh?" Tiredness dragged at her muscles as she pushed herself to a sitting position.

"Wei is a Dark Mage," said Carina. "Darius figured it out."

"*What*?!"

"Please, trust me. You know I don't bullshit. Hurry up. We have to wake the others."

For a second, Parthenia wondered if she was dreaming. Was her subconscious reacting to Kamil's insistence that they stay on Magog?

"Kai Wei's a *Dark Mage*?" she repeated stupidly. But before Carina answered, she believed her. She'd liked the man at first. He was so friendly and affable, but as she'd gotten to know him she'd sensed an undercurrent of self-centeredness and arrogance in his nature. Every conversation he'd taken part in he'd dominated, and he never talked about anyone else personally, as if he had no real friends. Then yesterday's event had been the icing on the cake.

"Okay," she said over Carina's attempt to explain. "I get it. Just give me a minute to get changed."

Carina moved away from the bed. "Don't forget your elixir."

Parthenia saw Darius was in her room, too, standing near the door.

"I'm going to wake Kamil," Carina said.

Taking Darius with her, she left.

Why had Wei really brought them there? They were alone on his island in the clouds. What was he planning to do? Had everything he'd told them about living on Magog as mages been a lie?

Parthenia climbed out of bed, turned on the light, and reached for her clothes, which she'd folded and piled on a chair.

She grabbed the hem of her pajama shirt, ready to pull it off over her head, but a small noise in the room made her turn around.

Kai Wei was standing there, one eyebrow lifted.

"Don't let me stop you," he said.

She spun around, scanning the room. Where had she put her elixir? The canister was next to her bed.

But Wei was too fast. He strode to her in three quick steps and grasped her wrist with vicious strength.

In his other hand he was holding a bottle. His eyes not leaving her face, he took a drink.

"Carina!" Parthenia yelled, trying to jerk her arm from his grip.

The bedroom door opened.

She saw her sister's dismayed face, and then she was somewhere else, somewhere dark and stuffy. Wei was still holding onto her.

"Now to get your brother and sister," he said.

As he spoke, his grip slackened.

Parthenia launched herself at him, throwing a wild punch that met flesh and bone.

Wei grunted. She heard him stumble and hit the floor. Falling to her knees, she reached out blindly, feeling for his bottle of elixir.

"*Bitch!*" muttered Wei between his teeth.

She could hear him scrabbling away from her. She crawled

after him. Her hand hit his foot, and she quickly grabbed his ankle.

All she had to do was to get the elixir, but she had to be fast or he would Transport out of there.

She released her hold on him, brought her legs forward, and gave a sharp kick at her estimated target.

The heel of her foot sank into something soft and yielding.

Wei went silent except for some soft groaning.

Parthenia crawled toward the sound. Her questing hands found the Dark Mage curled into a ball of quiet agony. Frantically, she patted his body. Where was the elixir?

She discovered an arm and followed it down to the hand, but it was empty.

Wei was beginning to recover from her blow, his groaning becoming louder.

He cursed.

Suddenly, her hair was in his grasp. He wrenched her head backward and punched her hard in the face once, twice, three times, before letting go of her.

Utterly dazed, Parthenia collapsed. Hot liquid poured from her nose and down the sides of her face. The pain brought tears to her eyes.

She swept out a hand, still trying to find the elixir, but it met nothing except wet, carpeted floor. Some of the elixir must have spilled from Wei's bottle. She listened, but all she could hear was her own panting.

The Dark Mage had gone.

28

"*S hit!*" Carina exclaimed as she watched her sister disappear with Wei.

"Parthenia!" Darius yelled. He ran into the empty room and turned in a circle. "She's gone! He took her! Carina, we have to get Parthenia back!"

Kamil emerged from his suite, sleepy eyed. Carina had opened his door when Parthenia had called out. The noise must have woken him.

"We will," Carina replied to Darius. "Don't worry."

Her plan to Transport everyone out of the mansion without Wei's knowledge had fallen to pieces.

"What's going on?" asked Kamil in confusion, smoothing his ruffled hair.

"Wei has taken Parthenia," Carina explained.

"What? Why?" As if to assure himself of the truth of what she was saying, he peered into Parthenia's suite.

"Wei is a Dark Mage, and—"

"A what?"

"A...Look, never mind. What you need to know is Kai Wei has an ulterior motive for bringing us here. I don't know what it is, and I don't need to know. We have to get out of here as fast as we can. You have to wake up Hsiao, Halliday, and Justus, and..."

Carina slapped her forehead. Now that Wei knew they were on to him and would try to leave, her plan of asking Poppy to pick them up at the estate under the cover of night might not work. The starwhale was a living creature. The Dark Mage could kill her with a single Cast.

Kamil was watching her.

"Wake up the others, and meet us at...at the entrance of the tunnel leading to the hangar."

"Are you sure Wei's taken Parthenia?" asked Kamil. "We're his guests. Why would he do that? Maybe she's just gone for a walk."

"I *saw* him take her," Carina replied. "He Transported her and himself away somewhere, and I'm pretty sure he'll be back soon for—"

Wei appeared in the corridor behind Kamil. The man's demeanor had transformed. His expression now oozed hatred.

Kamil's eyes widened as he looked at Carina. Following the direction of her gaze, he turned.

One look at Wei was apparently all it took to convince Kamil that Carina's assessment of the mage was correct. He began to back up, but then he halted.

"Leave him to us," Carina told him. "Do as I said. We'll be there as soon as we can."

"Where's Parthenia?" Kamil demanded. "If you've hurt her, I'll—"

Wei's attention had been focused on Carina, but Kamil's words distracted him. He looked at the young man, and his features twisted with contempt. His hand rose, bringing the bottle he was carrying to his lips.

"Kamil, run!" Carina yelled.

But the young man only began to stalk on rigid limbs toward Wei.

"Kamil!" shouted Carina.

What would Wei do? Would he Split him? Mages were useful, but the non-mage members of her party held no value for the Dark Mage.

Wei closed his eyes, but at the exact same moment, Kamil vanished. There hadn't been enough time for Wei to Cast.

What had happened?

When the Dark Mage opened his eyes, he glared at the empty space where Kamil had stood, looking as puzzled as Carina felt.

"*What* did you do?!" he roared.

Small, soft hands gripped her hips. Darius had moved behind her. She looked down to see him peek out fearfully at the mage.

"Did you Transport Kamil somewhere?" she asked him.

"Uh huh," he quietly replied.

"Good job."

Carina returned her attention to Wei.

"Look, I don't know what weird setup it is you have here, or why you want us to stay, but we're not interested. We're leaving Magog. Bring Parthenia back, and we'll go. That'll be the end of it. No one will get hurt."

Wei snorted with derision. "*I* won't get hurt, that's for sure."

"Where's my sister?" Carina pressed.

Then she realized she didn't need his answer. Reaching behind her, she felt for Darius's arm and squeezed it, hoping he would understand.

The Dark Mage scowled at her, no trace of his former charm remaining.

She could almost see the wheels of his mind turning as he tried to figure out what to do.

There was no point in him Transporting them to whatever place he'd put Parthenia. They were carrying elixir, and they would naturally Transport themselves and their sister right out of there. Carina also guessed he wouldn't try to kill them. Their powers were still useful to him, though now they were on to him he would have to force them to do his bidding.

If Darius had acted on her signal, Wei's hesitation was about to cost him dearly.

The Dark Mage vanished, along with the corridor and everything else around her. She was in darkness, but still inside the house.

She spun around and felt for Darius before grabbing the boy into a hug.

"Well done! You knew I wanted you to Transport us. Where are we?"

"In the dining room," he replied. "It's the place I remember best."

"Boy, am I glad to see you guys," said Kamil. "Though maybe 'see' isn't the right word."

"You're coming with us," Carina said. "We need to collect the others and Parthenia, and then get out of here."

"You know where Parthenia is?" asked Kamil.

"No, but I know how to find her."

Guessing that Wei might have security sensors everywhere in his home and he would soon arrive, Carina knew she had to work fast.

"Darius," she said. "You still have those items everyone gave you in your bag, right?"

"Yes!" he replied, realization of her intention in his tone. "I'll Locate Parthenia."

"No, I'll do it," said Carina. "But not yet. Let's get the others first."

"Oh, okay."

Darius sounded disappointed, but her plan was the safest way. She silently thanked the stars for her foresight in asking all the others to give her brother something that belonged to them so that, if he became separated from the group, he would be able to find them again.

"Come over here, quickly, Kamil," Carina urged.

Next, she asked Darius to Locate Hsiao and Transport them to her room.

Each Cast her brother made would use up precious elixir, but they'd both brought along plenty. She hoped that, once they'd escaped, they wouldn't need to Cast much more.

A FEW MINUTES LATER, everyone in their party except Parthenia was standing in the tunnel that led to the hangar where Wei kept his glider. There hadn't been time to explain to the three who'd been most recently awoken exactly what was happening, and now they stood in dazed disbelief at their sudden relocation.

Carina still had no time for explanations. She would have to leave them to Kamil and Darius.

"I'm going to get Parthenia," she told the group.

"Wait, I'll come too!" Darius exclaimed.

"No, I want you to stay here with everyone else. What did she give you?"

A grumpy frown marring his young features, Darius reached into his bag and brought out a comb.

Carina took it and held it as she Located her sister.

From the shadowy mental map she could see in her mind's eye, it appeared Wei had put Parthenia in the place he did his Casting for Magog's government—if what he'd told them was true. She'd been there a couple of times and could remember its layout. It was the obvious place: the room had no windows and little inside it that could be used as a weapon.

She took another drink of elixir.

"I'll be back soon," she said.

The instant the scene she saw switched to darkness, she called out, "Parthenia! Quick, grab me, and I'll—"

Uhhh!

Something had slammed into her.

She landed hard on her backside.

But she'd been expecting the attack, and she held on tight to her elixir canister. She swung the container around, hoping to hit Wei. She'd guessed correctly that he would go to where he was keeping Parthenia and wait for her there, knowing she wouldn't leave without her sister.

"Parthenia!" she yelled, but there was no answer. Wei must have gagged her.

Then the Dark Mage turned on the lights.

Her sister was sitting on the floor in the corner of the room, her knees drawn up and her ankles and wrists tied. A length of cloth was tightly bound around her face. She looked at Carina with frightened eyes.

Wei loomed over Carina. He motioned toward himself with the fingertips of one hand.

"Give me your elixir."

"Like hell I will," Carina retorted.

Would she have time to Cast before he could stop her?

Her gaze flicked to Parthenia.

"You'll never escape Magog," said Wei. "Your space-faring creature is far away, and wherever you go in Japheth, the Mayor's Watch will find you. You might as well give up now." The Dark Mage's expression softened, and traces of his previous cultured manner returned. "Let's not quarrel. I admit I could have been more forthright about the role of mages here, but I wasn't lying when I said you could have a very pleasant existence on my home world."

"I don't give a shit what you're doing on Magog," replied Carina.

The way she crouched on the floor, her hands were

partially concealed from Wei. Making the slightest of movements, she began to unscrew the lid of her canister.

"If you feel the need to dissemble, it's clearly something disgusting," she continued, "and we don't want any part of it."

"Well, whether you want to or not, you *are* going to be part of it!" Wei lunged at her, hands grasping for her elixir.

The canister was open. The impact of Wei's body knocked the lid from Carina's hand and slopped liquid out of the container.

She'd put her legs up, trying to kick him away, but the tall man had a long reach and, despite her pummeling his gut with her feet, he managed to grab the wet canister.

Carina grunted with effort as Wei tried to wrest the elixir from her grasp. She was holding the top and he had the bottom, and the tension created was slowly turning the container on its side. Elixir was running out in a thin stream. His other hand was occupied with trying to force her legs down. The canister was moving away from her, and she was losing her grip on the slippery surface. In another moment, he would have it.

She changed tactics. She bent down so her face neared the stream of elixir.

Wei saw what she was trying to do. His free hand left her legs, made a fist, and arced in toward her head.

Precious liquid ran into her mouth.

At the same time, Wei punched her in the jaw.

Her head jerked to the side and blackness encroached, but she managed to keep her mouth closed.

She focused her gaze on Parthenia, closed her eyes, and then she Cast.

29

J ackson put both his hands on the table, his prosthetic one making a soft *clunk*.

"We should have left them to the Regians," he said. "*That's* what we should have done. We were too soft. Now look where it's got us."

The merc had been pacing backward and forward, looking both frustrated and worried. He rubbed his stubble and set off on his pacing again. "Cadwallader would have left them to be larva food."

"Would he?" Bryce asked. "Really? Even he wasn't that hard-hearted, surely."

He was seated at the table in the same room where he'd held the meeting with Rebane, deciding with Jackson their next step in dealing with the Lotacryllans' insurrection.

"Huh," retorted Jackson. "*You* didn't know him when the Black Dogs first formed. In those days, he might have left *us* to be larva food. But maybe you're right. He'd lightened up a bit in recent times."

"Well, Cadwallader isn't here now," said Bryce. "It's up to us to figure out how to retrieve Jace and Calvaley unharmed."

After Rebane had left the meeting the previous day, Bryce had explained to Calvaley, Jace, and Jackson his reasoning behind his decision to set Pappu free. He'd grown suspicious about the Lotacryllan's constant pushing to release the giant, and wondered what it meant. He'd figured that if he gave in to Rebane's demand, it might act as a trigger, prompting the Lotacryllans to show their hand. If they intended to mutiny, it was better to find that out now than to discover it when they were all halfway to Earth and most of the mercs would be in Deep Sleep.

He'd wanted to give them enough rope to hang themselves.

That part of the plan had worked like a charm, though they'd acted faster than he'd anticipated. It was lucky he'd immediately stationed incognito guards to protect the kids.

He'd thought the bearded men would wait until the *Bathsheba* was refueled before making their move. Even if they succeeded in taking the ship, her fuel tanks were empty, and they had no way to communicate with the starwhales, though perhaps they thought Jace could.

The mage's offer to act as 'bait' had also worked. He'd been brave, deliberately staying alone in his cabin, expecting the Lotacryllans to take him hostage. But they'd also seized Calvaley. Bryce hadn't been expecting that. Getting the old man back safely was an added complication.

His other mistake had been assuming the Lotacryllans would retreat to the *Peregrine*. It was their ship, after all, their home ground to defend, and he'd thought they must have weapons aboard it, secretly stashed somewhere.

That guess had been wrong. The Lotacryllans had taken Deck Three, where an armory was located. They probably intended to force Jace to Unlock the door. He would refuse, of course, and Bryce hated to think what they might be doing to the man at that very moment. Even without Jace's help they might be able to break into the armory, given enough time.

"We've got to go in through the service tunnels," Jackson said. "It's the only way. We can't use the elevators. They only hold a few people, and there's nowhere to run if things start to go bad."

"It's not the only way," replied Bryce. "Ferne and Oriana could transport mercs to the deck a few at a time."

"But it's the same problem," countered Jackson. "There's no avenue of retreat."

"The Lotacryllans are not armed. We know that because if they were, they'd be attacking us right now. They might over-whelm a single fire team, but not successive groups of armed mercs. What worries me more is what they'll do when they realize they're losing."

Jackson grimaced. "Kill the hostages."

"Exactly," said Bryce. "We need to find out where they're holding Jace and Calvaley, go in and...*Stars*! It's simple. The kids can do it."

"What?" Jackson exclaimed. "No way! We can't send the kids in there, whether they're mages or not."

"That isn't what I mean."

Bryce opened a comm to Ferne.

THE TWINS TURNED up wearing matching outfits of brilliant blue. This time, it was Oriana who wore a suit, while Ferne had wrapped a short sarong around his waist, which hung down over blue leggings.

From their cheerful expressions, Bryce figured no one had fully explained the situation to them. When he told them that Jace and Calvaley had been kidnapped by the rebelling Lotacryllans, their faces fell.

"No!" Oriana blurted.

"So *that's* why you wanted us to Lock our door," Ferne said.

"You want us to help fight them? We brought elixir, like you asked." He held up a bottle in each hand.

"We need you to find the hostages for us," said Bryce. "You can find them, right?"

"Easy peasy," Ferne replied. "We just need something that belongs to them. Oriana can go and search Jace's cabin and I'll go to Calvaley's."

"No, stay here," Jackson said. "I'll order a couple of mercs to do it."

As the merc spoke, a comm arrived for Bryce. When he saw who it was from, he held up a hand for attention and then set the comm to broadcast room-wide.

"Rebane," he said, "Jace and Calvaley better still be alive, or you and your men will be leaving this ship through the garbage chutes."

"The mage and the old man aren't dead—yet," replied Rebane. "But they soon will be if you don't hand over control of the *Bathsheba*. We want you all to go to your old ship. You have five minutes. The hostages stay with us until you're aboard, then we'll give them over and set your ship adrift. If you aren't in your ship after five minutes, we kill one hostage. Then you'll have another five minutes before we kill the other one."

"Have you considered you might be overestimating how important those two men you're holding are to us?" asked Bryce. "We might let you kill them. Then what are you going to do?"

Oriana and Ferne gasped.

Bryce gave a little shake of his head to show them he was bluffing before continuing, "We've taken you guys down before and we'll do it again. And this time we'll space you."

"You got lucky before," Rebane replied, "and caught us off-guard. I'll admit we underestimated you, but we won't make the same mistake twice. Go to your ship. You'll be picked up eventually, and no one has to die. Think of it as a thank you for taking us along when you left the Regian planet."

"Taking you along?!" Jackson spluttered. "We *saved* you. If it wasn't for us you'd be having your guts eaten out right now. And this is how you pay us back? Fucking scum. We should have left you there to rot."

When Rebane replied, his tone was soft and quiet. "You'd better watch what you say. Words can hurt more than you might think."

A moment of silence passed.

"Rebane?" said Bryce. "Rebane, we need to talk about—"

"No, no, please. You don't have to..." said a voice over the comm.

Jace.

"Ferne, Oriana," Bryce barked, "get out."

The twins were wide-eyed with horror, frozen in position.

"Get out of here!"

Jackson pushed them toward the door, and Bryce gave the command to switch the comm back to person-to-person, but the twins were not outside before they heard Jace cry out.

The door slid shut, and Jace's wail continued in Bryce's ear only. His gut contracted in dismay.

"Rebane!" he snapped.

Jackson's eyes were ablaze as he turned from the door.

"Dead," he said. "They're all dead."

30

The problem was, if they Transported to Japheth, the Mayor's Watch would soon apprehend them, as Wei had kindly pointed out. Carina doubted that Ronny, Vasn, or Malte would be half so polite this time around. She and the others would never make it to the spaceport, and even if they did, Wei's people clearly ran the place and would send them right back to the island mansion.

The only alternative was to Transport to the surface and ask Poppy to pick them up there. But where would the space creature land in that sea of green? Nothing but trees had covered the land they'd seen on the glider flight. The only open space had been at the shoreline, where she'd seen thirty meters or so of beach leading down to the ocean.

How far away was the coast? She couldn't remember, and though she could take a guess, if she got it wrong she might Transport them all into the water, possibly kilometers from shore.

"Do either of you two remember how far it is to the ocean from here?" she asked Parthenia and Darius.

"Nope," Darius replied.

"I don't even remember which direction it's in," said Parthenia, still rubbing her wrists where Wei had tied them.

"I do," said Hsiao, "but I'm hazy on the distance. Wei's little stunt that nearly got us all killed was quite the distraction."

Carina peered into the darkness of the tunnel ahead, where the motion-sensing lights remained off. It wouldn't take Wei long to find their location. He probably had cameras and sensors all over his estate. They had to get out of there fast, but they couldn't afford to make mistakes. They only had Darius's elixir supply, and he'd already used up quite a bit of it.

Transporting to the shoreline was too risky, and walking there through the jungle on the surface would take days, assuming they didn't die of thirst or hunger along the way.

Then the answer hit her.

"Darius, can you Transport us all to the hangar?"

"Uh huh," he replied.

"Cool," Hsiao said to Carina. "I like your thinking, and the answer is yes."

Darius looked from person to person. "Are you ready, everyone?"

"We're ready, kid," Halliday replied. "Do your stuff."

DARIUS TRANSPORTED them to the center of the hangar. Carina briefly saw darkness before the lights sensed their arrival and blinked on. The glider squatted like a bird about to leap into flight, facing the hangar doors. The space felt vast after the claustrophobic confines of the tunnel, and outside the wind was howling.

Hsiao briefly grimaced, then the pilot's expression turned neutral. She was concerned about the wind but trying to hide it, Carina guessed.

"Are you still okay with this?" she asked Hsiao.

The woman paused a beat before replying, "If things go bad, can the little guy move us all onto the land before we crash?"

"There'll be a second or two lag," Carina said. "He'll need some notice." She also wasn't sure if Darius could Transport people who were moving fast or, when Transported, they would retain their velocity on arrival. As far as she could recall, she'd only ever Transported people who were standing still. Whether Darius could get them out of the falling glider or not, it might not make any difference.

"I'll do what I can," said Hsiao.

"I know you will," replied Carina. "Let's go everyone!" She took Darius's hand and began to jog toward the glider.

They were halfway there when Kai Wei appeared near the hangar doors.

Halliday swore, then said, "I'll deal with him. You all carry on."

"No," said Carina. "Give me your canister, Darius."

Her brother tried to pass it to her, but he was still running and the container slipped from his grasp and hit the floor before bouncing and rolling away. Carina ran after it.

Wei was already lifting his bottle to his lips.

Kamil began to yell.

He altered direction and then pelted full speed toward Wei, his yell growing louder and louder.

"*No!*" Carina yelled. "Come back here! It's too dangerous!"

But the distance between them was too great. The mage had already closed his eyes before Kamil reached him.

Carina tensed in anguish, clutching Darius's elixir. She hadn't had time to do anything. What Cast had Wei made? Was he going to Split Kamil? She berated herself for allowing him and Parthenia to come along. She hadn't needed them there. Why had she agreed?

The others had nearly made it to the glider.

She ran after them, fearful of seeing Kamil die an agonizing death any second.

The Dark Mage's eyes opened as Kamil crashed into him, smashing him against the hangar doors, which resounded with a metallic clang. The two men briefly tussled, then Kamil managed to get on top. He punched Wei in the face again and again.

"That's for Parthenia, you bastard!"

Carina was confused. What Cast had Wei made? Why hadn't he defended himself when he saw Kamil run at him?

Hsiao had already raced up the steps to the glider door and was opening it, so Wei hadn't Cast Lock.

Then, faint in the noise of the wind, she heard the familiar hiss of pulse fire.

Justus screamed. He was halfway up the steps, but as he cried out tumbled from them and fell heavily, smacking into the concrete floor.

Carina whirled around to see the source of the firing.

Ronny, Vasn, and Malte were walking slowly toward them, rifles at their shoulders.

Wei's Cast had Transported them there. In the time since Carina and Parthenia had escaped him, he must have comm'd them about the situation and told them to bring weapons.

Halliday was next to be hit, but he was halfway inside the glider, and the round skimmed his leg. He hollered, but Carina didn't think he was badly hurt. The same couldn't be said for Justus. The Lotacryllan writhed in agony, one of his arms and half his side burned.

"Parthenia, Darius," said Carina, "get into the glider."

Parthenia grabbed their brother and partly dragged, partly carried him up the steps.

Carina ducked under the fuselage. The glider's rear wheel gave her some cover.

The Mayor's Watch seemed to have been aiming at the non-mages, but as soon as Carina moved under the glider they began to sprint toward her, firing as they ran.

Their motion caused their shots to go wide, and some hit the aircraft. The paint blistered and smoked.

She had to get rid of them soon or the only means of escape for herself and the others would be destroyed. She squatted right behind the wheel, making herself as small as she could, and took a drink of elixir. She closed her eyes. Would her Cast take effect before the Mayor's Watch officers reached her? It would be close.

As she opened her eyes, she found herself staring directly into Ronny's as he ran up. Vasn and Malte were running on each side of him, half a second behind.

Ronny slowed down, smirked, and took aim.

Then he vanished.

Vasn and Malte disappeared, too.

Transported somewhere outside the hangar, in the stormy gale, all three were falling to their deaths.

Carina darted to the bottom of the steps where Justus still lay, now barely conscious.

"Come on, get up," she said, hauling at the large man. His eyes opened and focused on her, and he made an effort to move. Gasping in pain, he managed to rise to his feet. Carina put his arm over her shoulder and helped him up the steps. He made it a few steps inside the glider, and then collapsed.

Hsiao was already in the cockpit. Halliday was seated at the front of the passenger cabin, clutching his right calf, his face pale and sweaty. Darius and Parthenia sat on the other side of the aisle.

"I need those doors open!" Hsiao called out. "They're not responding to commands."

"Where's Kamil?" Parthenia asked.

"*Shit.*" Carina turned to go out again.

"I'll come with you," said Parthenia.

"No," replied Carina, "stay here."

But her sister ignored her and followed her down the steps.

As they rounded the nose of the glider, Wei and Kamil came rolling toward them, still locked in battle. Both men's faces and hands were bloody and their clothing torn.

"Unlock the hangar doors," Carina told her sister, thrusting the elixir canister into her hands. "I'll help Kamil."

Wei's bottle of elixir lay meters away on its side, a puddle around its mouth. Carina was tempted to run and get it, just for the small amount of fluid that might remain inside, but the Dark Mage had his hands around Kamil's throat and was throttling him.

Carina stepped over to the men, drew back her foot, and kicked Wei in the head, jolting him off Kamil. Wei slumped to the floor but then, his hands reaching for his head, he rose halfway to his feet. He staggered a few steps, his knees seemed to buckle, and he collapsed.

A heavy *clunk* sounded from the hangar doors.

Kamil didn't move. Purple fingermarks were already rising on his neck, and his face was puffy and dark.

Had Wei killed him?

Carina knelt down and grasped the man's shoulders, shaking him, guilt racking her. "Kamil!"

The hangar doors began to slowly trundle apart. Wind gusted in through the widening gap. Outside, the night was starless.

Parthenia arrived and dropped to her knees on the other side of Kamil. She collapsed onto him, burying her face in his chest, and Carina heard her muffled wail.

His eyelids lifted, and one of his hands rose to his neck, as if checking that the choking pressure had gone.

"He's alive," Carina said. "Parthenia, he's alive! Come on, help me get him to the glider."

But as she spoke, Wei rose into view behind her sister.

31

The Lotacryllans were holding Jace and Calvaley separately on Deck Three. Jace was inside a single cabin at one end of the passage that ran the length of the deck, and Calvaley was being held in a storage room at the other end, near a closed-off elevator.

Bryce checked the time. It had taken two minutes to bring a possession belonging to each of the hostages to Oriana and Ferne, and for them to Cast Locate. While they'd been doing that, he and Jackson had suited up and armed themselves. Armed mercs also waited in the passage.

Only three minutes of the five Rebane had allotted them to move everyone into *Duchess* remained.

If only Calvaley were with them and not lying trussed up somewhere below, guarded by the Lotacryllans. Bryce had a feeling the former Sherrerr admiral would have figured out a rescue plan in a trice.

The twins were also studying the 3D holo of the deck.

"We can Transport however many mercs you want down there," Oriana said, "but only six at a time, with a few seconds' delay between each group."

"We can also advance some teams down the service tunnels," said Jackson.

"They'll be guarding those for sure," said Bryce. "They've separated Jace and Calvaley on purpose. If it looks like we're going to succeed in rescuing one, they'll threaten to kill the other one to make us back off."

Jackson grunted his agreement. "We've got to strike both areas at once."

Bryce scanned the plan. He didn't have any doubts about the Black Dogs' ability to defeat the Lotacryllans. They'd done it before, and this time around the bearded men probably weren't even armed. But he didn't want Jace or Calvaley to die. Jace's cry of pain when Rebane had hurt him had been weak, as if he'd already suffered torture. Rebane clearly wasn't going to stop at anything to get his way, or exact his revenge if he didn't.

The trick was going to be in going in so fast and brutally, the Lotacryllans wouldn't have time to get their revenge. Three mercs arriving at each site at a time wouldn't accomplish that. They needed more than the twins' help to get them there.

Then he spotted something on the plan where the passage ended at the ship's hull.

"Two minutes," Jackson said.

"Should we start Transporting soldiers now?" asked Ferne.

Bryce reached out and touched the object he'd noticed on the plan of Deck Three.

A label appeared, stating a single word: *Airlock.*

"Holy shit," said Jackson. "That's it! I'll get on it." He ran a few steps toward the door, and then raced back to the plan. "That's where they're keeping the mage, right?" he asked, taking another look at the plan. Without waiting for an answer, he returned to the door, already speaking into his comm.

"It looks like I'll be rescuing Calvaley," Bryce said to the twins. "I want you to Transport me and five mercs directly inside the storage room where the Lotacryllans are holding him. After we've arrived, Transport six more directly outside, in case they manage to take us down. Carry on Transporting mercs to Deck Three. They'll figure it out from there."

He wasn't in any doubt the enemy soldiers would be prepared for exactly what he was going to do, not because they were smart, but because there was no alternative.

"That sounds really dangerous," said Oriana.

"We have a big advantage," Bryce replied. "All we need is speed."

"We should come with you," Ferne said, "to Heal the wounded soldiers."

"Absolutely not," said Bryce. "We won't be able to keep you safe."

"What if they've broken into the armory?" Oriana asked.

"Let's hope they haven't." Bryce picked up his pulse rifle.

A comm arrived from Rebane.

Without waiting for Bryce to speak, the Lotacryllan said, "I want to see a feed of the Black Dogs inside their ship."

"We aren't all in there yet," Bryce replied. "We still have one minute." He made eye contact with the twins and jerked his head in the direction of the door.

"Bullshit," Rebane spat. "You've had plenty of time. Send me the feed, now!"

Bryce sped out of the room, Ferne and Oriana hurrying after him.

WHEN HE APPEARED in the room where the Lotacryllans were holding Calvaley, the first thing he noticed was that both Rebane and Pappu were guarding the former Sherrerr admiral. They and several other bearded men had formed a quarter circle in one of the room's corners. More of the enemy were scattered around the space, about twenty or so men.

The second thing he noticed was that they were wearing improvised armor, apparently hastily printed somewhere on the deck. They'd even fashioned helmets with visors.

As Bryce was registering these facts and lifting his rifle to take aim, the Lotacryllans rushed the mercs. He got off two shots, both hitting Pappu square in his stomach, before someone smashed into his side, throwing him to the floor.

Instantly, the man's hands were on his rifle, but Bryce had been expecting that and he maintained an iron grip, wrestling his attacker for possession of his weapon. The Lotacryllan was on top of him. He brought up his knee sharply into the man's abdomen and saw his face contort with pain.

Taking his moment, Bryce pushed the Lotacryllan off and leapt up. He fired at the man's head at point blank range, melting the printed material onto his face. A muted scream came through the gooey, smoking mess, and then someone else crashed into Bryce.

He found himself down once more, this time under a heavier weight. He fought and twisted, catching a glimpse of a face.

Rebane.

One of his hands gripped the muzzle of Bryce's rifle, forcing it away from him, while the other reached for the stock. Bryce tried to wrench the weapon away from him, but he didn't succeed. Rebane's face was a picture of grimacing, vein-popping effort as he grappled for the rifle.

Bryce couldn't move. All his strength was concentrated on not letting go of his weapon. He also couldn't see what else was happening. Were the Black Dogs gaining the advantage? It should have been easier than this. Where were the mercs Oriana and Ferne had Transported to outside the room?

Summoning an extra burst of energy, Bryce jerked the rifle from Rebane's grip. He tried to bring it around to shoot at the man, but the Lotacryllan pressed close against him, not giving him room to fire, crushing his weapon against his chest.

Bryce tried to turn one way and then the other, but he couldn't shift Rebane. They were visor to visor, the man's wild eyes staring into his.

Suddenly, he knew what he had to do. While pretending to continue to try to throw the Lotacryllan off, he edged his rifle up between them. The space was extremely tight, and his armor meant he could barely feel the weapon's movement. But after several long seconds of struggle, he felt the end of the muzzle clunk against the bottom of his helmet.

Rebane must have felt it too because his eyes snapped wide, and Bryce felt the pressure of the man's weight begin to ease.

He swung his head to the right, and fired.

Hot pain seared his jaw and ear, and his helmet was filled with the stench of burned hair.

Rebane's body sagged on top of him. He pushed at the limp form and managed to slide out from under it. He stood up. The Lotacryllan remained face downward, blood oozing from his makeshift helmet, which had proven no match for the real thing.

Not that his own helmet was in such great shape. Half of his visor was blackened from the pulse round, and the HUD wasn't operating. He had to move his head around to get a proper view of the room. The fighting seemed to have stopped.

What he saw next caused him to unclip his helmet locks and take it off.

Holding his helmet in one hand and his rifle in the other, he walked to the group of mercs standing over a body on the floor.

Looking older than ever and fragile, little more than thin,

pale skin over bones, Calvaley lay curled in a fetal position. His throat had been cut, and the blood he lay in had dried and turned brown.

The Lotacryllans had murdered him not long after they took him hostage.

32

"Take Kamil," Carina told her sister, deeply relieved the young man was still alive.

Wei was slowly walking toward them, blood dripping from his nose and eyebrow, his upper lip and right eye puffed up after his fight. He blinked as if struggling to focus, but his expression was murderous.

Parthenia looked over her shoulder, following the direction of Carina's gaze, and then quickly stooped down to help her boyfriend.

Carina stood and clenched her fists as she sized up the approaching Dark Mage.

Wei was bigger than her but he had to be tired already from fighting Kamil. All she had to do was to knock him out or incapacitate him for a short while, just until her companions and herself could escape in the glider.

No, that isn't enough.

They'd left some of their possessions behind in the mansion. Wei would use them to Cast Locate after they left. As long as the Dark Mage remained alive, he would always be able to find them.

With Parthenia's support, Kamil was slowly rising to his feet.

A blast of wind roared through the open hangar doors, nearly blowing Carina off her feet. Wei leaned into it, narrowing his eyes.

Parthenia and Kamil began to move away.

"We could have done so much together," Wei yelled over the gale's moan. "You could have had so much. Authority, power, a life of luxury."

Carina yelled back, "Let us go peacefully, and I won't hurt you."

Wei twisted his head to one side and smiled wryly.

Then he ran at her.

Carina put her left leg back and raised her fists.

Parthenia and Kamil had only gone a couple of small steps. As Wei passed the pair he shoved Parthenia hard, propelling her and Kamil toward the hangar opening. She lost her hold on Kamil and he continued backward, his arms windmilling and legs faltering as he tried to regain his balance in his dazed state.

Parthenia screamed and leapt toward him, reaching out to grab his shirt, but snatching at empty air.

The back of Kamil's heel hit the low ledge, he overbalanced, and then, almost gracefully, tipped backward. In another heart-beat he was gone.

As Parthenia sent out an agonized cry, Wei slammed into Carina. Her concentration broken by Kamil's death and her sister's anguish, she landed hard, her spine smashing onto the floor.

Before she could do anything to protect herself, Wei's knees pinned her arms and his hands closed around her throat. His bruised and bloody visage hung above her, naked fury in his eyes.

She squirmed and struggled, trying to throw him off, but he was too heavy. The power of his knees grinding into her biceps was deadening her arms, but worse was the pressure building up in her head. She choked and kicked her legs, uselessly.

Blackness edged her vision.

Wei began to fade from sight.

Then just above her a dull *thunk* sounded, and, suddenly, the pressure on her throat was gone. A split second later it was gone from her arms, too. Her vision was returning.

Wei had disappeared.

The *thunk* sounded again, quickly followed by the splintering of glass.

"Help me," Parthenia called out. "Help me, Carina!"

Crunching her aching gut, she sat up.

Wei lay sprawled on his back, knocked out. The shattered glass of his elixir bottle lay scattered next to his head. Parthenia bent down and began to push his limp body to the edge of the hangar.

Carina crawled over, the blood returning to her arms in a painful tingle, and joined her sister in sliding Wei toward the drop off.

The wind battered them as they shifted the unconscious man closer to his doom. Parthenia was sobbing, her teardrops falling on her boyfriend's murderer.

Just another half a meter.

"We can do it," Carina said hoarsely.

The Dark Mage's eyelids fluttered, and he groaned.

Her sister gave a cry of pent up rage and thrust Wei hard, driving the man the remaining distance.

Another gust of wind blew in. Wei's eyes opened and then stretched wide.

Parthenia turned onto her back and braced both feet against his hip and thigh, trying to force him over the ledge. Carina locked her elbows and pushed his shoulder.

Wei was awake. His arms and legs moved, and he started to

fight against the pressure the sisters were exerting, but at the same moment his body began to roll.

"*No!*" the Dark Mage bellowed.

He was rotating into empty space.

They'd done it.

"Goodbye, Wei," panted Carina.

As he fell, his hand shot out, clutched at the ledge…and missed.

The night swallowed him.

FOR A MOMENT after Wei's death, Carina had wondered if their danger was now over, if the Dark Mage was their only threat on Magog, and if the three members of the Mayor's Watch had been his only subordinates. But she'd concluded that none of her hopes was likely to be true. The Dark Mage had spoken of his influence in the planet's government, and others in power had to know what was going on.

Magog would never be safe for them.

"Belt up!" Hsiao hollered from the pilot's cabin.

The glider began to roll forward.

Carina fastened her seat belt, scanning the cabin to check everyone else was doing the same. Halliday was sitting with Darius, helping him to fasten his belt. He saw Carina watching and gave her a thumbs up. Parthenia, looking devastated, had sat down next to Justus, who seemed to be unconscious due to the pain of his wound.

On her way back to the glider, she'd only just remembered to find the elixir canister she'd given to her sister when they'd gone to get Kamil. She'd snatched it from the floor before running to the aircraft.

She picked it up from her lap and gave the container a shake.

It was nearly empty. Her stomach sank.

Despite the small quantity of the precious liquid remaining, she attracted Parthenia's attention and then passed the elixir over. Healing Justus would distract her from her grief for a moment.

"This is going to be a wild ride," Hsiao called out. "Brace yourselves!"

Night was beginning to give way to one of Magog's swift dawns, but the windstorm was not abating. The glider bucked and landed with a judder as the wings rose on the gale even before she was airborne.

Carina saw Hsiao shake her head, then the pilot shouted, "Here we go!"

The glider left the hangar.

Immediately her nose lifted high and the aircraft was blown backward. Tipped back in her seat, Carina gripped the seat arms, expecting the glider to be smashed against the hangar roof. But somehow Hsiao managed to bring the nose down and urge the aircraft forward. Carina guessed the pilot was using the a-grav to help keep her steady.

To her right, the sky was rapidly paling. Below, the dark jungle stretched to the horizon in every direction. Carina could just make out the green mountain slopes that sat directly beneath Japheth. They were leaving them behind, venturing into the airspace over the flat land that led to the ocean.

The wind keened around them, causing the glider to rise and drop with sickening suddenness.

She contemplated asking Darius to Send to Poppy and ask her to meet them at the shore. She didn't know how far away the space creature was or how long it would take her to reach them. But she decided against it. She didn't know where they would end up and so she couldn't give Poppy a destination. Also, now that Wei was dead, she worried that Magog's government would be watching for a living starship entering their atmosphere.

She looked over at Justus. Parthenia had made her Cast, and the man's skin was back to normal under his charred clothes. Her sister was staring out her window, her eyes unfocused and her features blank.

Carina checked Halliday and Darius. The merc's look was stoical, but her brother had turned green. She understood exactly how he felt.

Turning to face forward again, she saw a dark cloud looming directly ahead. Hsiao seemed to be trying to navigate around it, but the cloud was vast.

A flash of blinding light zigzagged through it, almost instantaneously followed by an ear-splitting crack of thunder.

The cloud appeared to rush forward to meet them.

Lightning blazed again and thunder roared so loud the aircraft shook.

Suddenly, the glider jumped upward as if batted by a giant, invisible hand. Then it dropped so fast Carina lifted out of her seat, retained only by her belt. Over the noise of the air rushing past, she could hear Hsiao cursing.

Long seconds ticked away as the glider plummeted. Carina kept anticipating the moment the aircraft would rise again, but it never came. Inside the cabin, no one moved or spoke. Outside was only darkness within the enveloping cloud.

Hsiao looked back at Carina, her face stricken with fear.

She knew what the pilot wanted without the need for her to speak: Darius had to Transport them. They were about to crash.

She scanned for the elixir.

Parthenia was still holding it. She called her sister's name. Parthenia's head turned toward her, and Carina gestured to give the canister to Darius.

Suddenly, the cloud was gone. Through Parthenia's window,

Carina saw the wide jungle canopy racing up, already frighteningly close. A curtain of gray rain pelted down, the drumming of its drops on the aircraft and the vegetation rising above the noise of the wind.

It was too late. They were too close to the ground.

A Cast would never take effect in time to save them.

Then their precipitous descent stopped with a jerk. Carina found herself sitting normally in her seat again. But though the glider began flying forward, her trajectory still tended downward.

She skimmed the treetops. A second later her fuselage and wings began crashing through branches and leaves. The world became a chaos of rushing, breaking vegetation and shouts and screams in the cabin.

A sudden stop threw Carina forward.

Then she knew no more.

33

S omething was tickling her face, and her head felt heavy. She could hear a rhythmic swishing sound and the far off cries of animals.

Carina opened her eyes to a blurry, green scene. She was dreadfully hot. The tickling sensation seemed to be droplets of sweat running down her skin. Something was gripping her tightly across her hips.

Why were her arms over her head?

She blinked and swallowed. Memories of what had happened before she lost consciousness were leaking slowly into her mind. The glider had lost altitude, fast, dropping like a stone through a storm cloud.

They'd crashed in the jungle. That explained the green surrounding her and the very warm, very humid air, thick with the scent of decaying leaves.

What had happened to the others?

"Darius!" she called out, though her intended shout came out as a hoarse whisper. "Parthenia?"

As she spoke, she moved her arms, and realized they were above her head because she was upside down. The sensation of tightness over her hips was her seat belt, suspending her from her seat. That was why her head felt heavy.

The blurriness of her vision was resolving. Leaves and smashed vegetation grew distinct. She seemed to be outside in the jungle. What had happened to the glider, and Hsiao?

"Darius?" Her cry was thickened by a sob that welled up.

This trip to buy fuel had turned into a disaster. Were her brother and sister dead? What had happened to the rest of her party?

She tried to turn to look behind her, but her movement was restricted by her seat belt. She looked above her, which was downward, and saw brown earth, freshly dug out by the crashing aircraft. The glider's roof had been ripped off. The drop looked to be about a couple meters.

She fumbled at her belt, feeling for the catch. As she opened it, she tucked her head in to prepare for the impact.

Landing on her shoulders, the ground was soft and spongy and saved her from any serious harm. After taking a moment to recover, she stood up.

The fuselage of the glider lay behind her, or, rather, what remained of the fuselage. The seats at the rear had been entirely ripped away, like the front of the glider. All she could see was the mid-section, lying at a low angle with the ground.

The seats where Parthenia and Justus had been sitting were only a short distance above the soil. They were empty, and their seat belts hung free.

Darius and Halliday's seats had been bent backward and rested on the ground. They were empty too—except, no.

She drew in a breath.

Coated in the brown, torn-up soil, a pair of legs protruded into the aisle. Carina stepped closer, though she'd recognized the legs immediately. Peering between the seats, what she saw confirmed her fear: Halliday was dead, his neck broken.

She stood still for a few moments, gazing at the poor man's

body. He'd been a Black Dog for years before she'd joined, one of the oldest members of the band. He'd been a fierce fighter, and one of those who treated his fellow mercs like family—disrespectful but loyal to a fault.

Cadwallader and Atoi were dead, and now Halliday, too. How many more would die helping her to pursue her dream?

"Carina!"

A rustling of foliage, and Darius burst into the crash site. He ran toward her, and she took a few steps forward to meet him so he wouldn't see Halliday's body.

"Come back here!" Parthenia yelled, still invisible among the broken trees. Then her sister emerged, breathless, her face scratched and her hair full of dead leaves. "We were just coming back to get you," she said to Carina, "but Darius wouldn't wait with Hsiao. He ran off."

"Hsiao's alive?" Carina asked.

"Yes," replied Parthenia, "but I had to use the last of the elixir to Heal her. Justus is fine, too. He and I weren't injured. Halliday..."

"I know."

"That's why I didn't want Darius to come back here." Parthenia looked sadly at her brother.

"He's dead, isn't he?" Darius asked.

"Yes," Carina softly replied, taking his hand. "Come on, let's go."

Parthenia led the way through the jungle.

"When we couldn't see Hsiao," she said, "Justus and I decided to try and find her before getting you down. You didn't seem injured except for being knocked out. It was the right decision, I think. She's lost a lot of blood, but I think she'll be okay. We found Darius under Halliday. He'd leaned over him, protecting him when we crashed."

The glider cockpit lay a short walk away, so smashed up

Carina marveled that Hsiao had survived the crash. The aircraft's wings had disappeared.

In a small clearing another half a minute's walk distant, Justus was sitting with the pilot. The latter was lying on her side, her clothes were torn and soaked in blood, but she was conscious. Carina knelt down near her.

"I tried..." Hsiao said weakly.

"You did a great job," Carina said. "If you hadn't been flying us, we would have all died."

She knew how the pilot felt. She also had deaths on her conscience.

For the first time since the accident, she took a proper look at their surroundings. Through gaps in the canopy high above, she saw a blue, cloudless sky. The storm they'd flown through had passed, dripping foliage all around them the only remaining signs of its existence. From the intensity of the light, she guessed it was about midday.

Visibility at ground level was limited by the close-standing tree trunks to three or four meters.

"Do you remember how far we were from the coast when we crashed?" she asked Hsiao.

"At a rough guess, I'd say ten to fifteen kilometers."

"And were we still facing in the right direction?" Carina also asked. "I mean, is the wreck of the glider pointing the way we should go?"

"Honestly, I don't know," the pilot replied.

Carina checked the sky again. If her estimation of the time was correct, they had about an hour and a half until sunset. She strongly doubted they would make it to the ocean by then, especially not walking through heavy forest and with Hsiao, who was still very weak.

There was also the problem that they didn't know for sure where the coast lay, though maybe when the sun had lowered in the sky a little they might have a better idea.

And they'd run out of elixir. If they could find a source of water and could start a fire, they could make more—she'd brought along a firestone and the other ingredients in case of an emergency—but though water probably wouldn't be hard to find after the recent rainstorm, lighting a fire with sodden wood could prove difficult.

"We should get moving," she said. "How are you feeling, Hsiao? Are you up to walking for a while?"

"Sure," the pilot replied, putting on a confident expression that didn't fool Carina for a minute. "I feel better already."

The heat was oppressive. Carina suggested that they take off all their clothing except the bare essentials on the top halves of their bodies, but bring the items along in case they were needed later.

"Can I take off my pants, too?" Darius asked.

"No, leave them on," she replied, taking off her jacket. "Creatures that bite might live in the undergrowth." She tied the arms of her jacket around her waist.

Justus helped Hsiao to stand, and when everyone was ready they set off.

NAVIGATING through the jungle was nearly impossible. Often they hit upon a patch of vegetation that was so thick not even Justus could penetrate it. They were forced to go around, and often the patches were tens of meters wide. Carina wasn't confident that when they reached the other side they maintained the same course. As they went on, she had a growing feeling they were getting irretrievably lost.

Meanwhile, the sunlight was rapidly fading. At first, Carina had been heartened by this, thinking that she would be able to figure out the direction of the coast if she could see the sun's position in the sky. But when she tried to climb a tree to take a look, the branches at the top were too thin to support her weight and she couldn't climb high enough to look out of the canopy. Other trees she tried were the same, and she was forced to give up.

Hsiao looked to be on her last legs, too, though she tried her best to hide it. On the third occasion she lagged behind the group, Justus went back for her and insisted she climbed onto his back.

They'd been going for about an hour, Carina guessed, and the sky had turned a darker blue, when she heard something different from the jungle sounds they'd gotten used to. The ubiquitous, repetitive squeak-squeak-squeak of a bird or other animal, the stridulation of insects, and the occasional explosion of movement as their approach spooked a creature ahead of them were all familiar, but this noise was new.

Carina raised her hand, signaling a halt.

Almost instantly, the sound stopped.

She swung around. It had been coming from behind them.

Justus relaxed his arms, allowing Hsiao to slide from his back. He nodded at Carina. He'd heard the noise, too.

"Wait here," she told the others.

Together, she and Justus walked softly in the direction they'd come.

She was sure the noise had been that of one or more people walking after them, presumably following them. She silently cursed the low visibility.

Who was on their trail? She didn't know anything about the Magogians who lived on the surface, except that they had to be poorer than the likes of Kai Wei. No one would choose to live in the hot, humid conditions if they had the option of residing among cool clouds.

Or were their stalkers associates of Wei? The wreckage of the glider was probably visible from the air, and they were traveling slowly. It wouldn't take long for fresh, provisioned trackers to catch up to them.

Suddenly, a scream sounded out behind them, and then, just as abruptly, it cut off.

"That was Parthenia!" Carina began to run back along the trail.

"Carina, wait!" shouted Justus.

She sped on, desperate to reach her sister.

It had been a trap. Their attackers had lured her and Justus away, splitting up their group.

Two figures stepped onto the track, one on each side.

Carina tried to stop, but she was going too fast. One of the figures reached out long, muscular arms and grabbed her. The other thrust a finger into her ear and popped out her comm. She felt arms tighten around her chest, locking her own to her sides. Then she was pushed to the ground. Strong hands gripped her ankles, forcing them together. A binding tightened around them, and then she was unceremoniously thrown onto her front while her arms were twisted behind her back.

Within seconds of hearing her sister scream, she found herself hogtied.

34

Parthenia stumbled and fell onto her knees, jerking the rope around her neck.

"Get up!" a Magogian man snapped.

But she was exhausted and desperately thirsty, and she didn't rise as fast as the man wanted. He grabbed her hair, yanked her to her feet, and roughly pushed her forward.

She trudged on.

Darius was in front of her, and Justus walked behind her in the line, pulling Hsiao on a makeshift litter. Since the Magogians had pounced on them as they waited for Carina and Justus to return from investigating the sound, they'd been going for hours, through sunset and the nighttime, and now dawn was approaching, silvering the trees' leaves.

Carina was walking behind Hsiao. At least, Parthenia hoped her sister was still there. She'd seen the Magogians cut Carina's ties and force her to stand before fastening a rope around her neck that joined her to Darius and Hsiao. They'd done the same to Justus, and then they'd set off.

Since then, their captors had refused to allow them to

speak. Poor Hsiao had said something to Carina and been punished with a blow to the head. After that, she'd been unable to walk, and the Magogians had made the litter to carry her from thin branches and leaves.

Who were the ten or twelve men and women walking alongside them? Now that the light was increasing, she could see them better. When she risked glances to each side, she saw Magogians who looked nothing like the people who dwelt in Japheth. The people forcing them on their march were only lightly clothed, and what they wore seemed to be made from animal hides, including their shoes.

Their hair was cut short all over their heads, even the women's, but whereas Wei's hair had been carefully styled, theirs looked as though it had been hacked off. Though they were clearly aggressive, the only weapons they carried were knives, which they thrust into sheaths at their hips.

Where were they going, and what would the Magogians do to them when they arrived? Not a word of explanation had been given. Wei was dead, and so were the members of the Mayor's Watch. Were they going to be put on trial for murder?

Her worries were legitimate, but Parthenia also knew she was trying to distract herself from thinking about Kamil.

Through the long, hot, night, as she'd trekked the jungle following the leader's light, her well of grief had overflowed. She'd sobbed, not caring that the others could hear her, until she'd cried herself dry. Kamil hadn't been perfect by any means, and neither was she, but she'd cared about him deeply.

And he'd cared about her, too. It had been for her sake he'd attacked Wei. It had been *her* name he'd shouted as he punched the Dark Mage, revenging the wrongs done to her. Kamil had given them time to get to the glider, so their escape was partly due to him. Whether he'd intended it or not, he'd given his life to help them.

Though they hadn't known each other long, and though their relationship had its problems, when she imagined a future without him a dark hole opened up inside her that she didn't think would ever be filled.

She wanted to cry again, but no tears would come. She'd stopped sweating, too, and her head thumped with pain. Putting each foot in front of the other was becoming a monumental effort. She knew she was going to fall again, soon, but there wasn't anything she could do about it.

Then the light the leader was carrying went out.

Sunlight was penetrating the canopy, illuminating the way ahead. Parthenia saw the back of Darius's head, which hung low. The poor kid. She wished she could say just a few words of comfort to him.

She could see the leader, too. He was putting away the lamp that he'd hung from a long flexible stick throughout the dark hours. His naked back was all muscle, carrying no fat.

Then she smelt an aroma that conjured up a perfect day, unbelievably recent—salt and the faint odor of decay. They had reached the coast!

The close, cloying jungle air was freshening, and the trees no longer grew so close.

She looked down. The deep brown, rich leaf mold of the jungle floor had turned lighter and coarser.

Hope that they'd finally reached their destination rose in her, and after walking another two or three minutes, it was fulfilled. Through tree trunks ahead she caught a glimpse of blue—not the pale blue of the morning sky, but the crystal blue of the ocean.

They were led out onto a beach of fine, silver sand and walked along it. After walking about a hundred and fifty meters, they turned a wide bend. A small settlement was revealed in the distance hugging the forest edge. Parthenia saw huts made from driftwood and large leaves, and a thin stream of smoke rising, quickly dissipated by the wind.

As they drew closer, she began to make out small figures—children, running between the huts and down to the water's edge before racing back up the beach.

In another few hundred meters they reached the habitation and walked between irregularly spaced huts until they arrived at an open, central area. The fire Parthenia had seen from afar burned here, bigger than it had seemed from its stream of smoke, and surrounded by stones.

Their troupe must have been seen approaching, for several of the village's inhabitants were awaiting them, seated on a large, woven floor covering spread out on the sand. They were older than the captors and dressed differently in regular clothes made of cloth.

The leader moved to the side, and Parthenia and the others were brought forward to stand in a line before the seated villagers.

"Please," Parthenia said, "can we have some water? My brother is only a child, and we've been walking for hours."

One of their captors strode toward her as if to strike her, but a villager raised his hand and said, "It's fine. Get them water."

The man who had spoken was younger than most of the villagers. His left arm hung at a strange angle and rested in his lap, as if he couldn't move it. Like the rest of those seated, his hair was longer and shaggier than that of the Magogians who had brought them there.

"Please, sit down," the man said.

With great relief, Parthenia dropped to her knees and then sat on her bottom. She would have gladly *lain* down. A bowl of water was thrust in front of her face. She grabbed it eagerly and began gulping the water down.

"Don't drink so fast," the man said to her. "You'll bring it up again, and water is scarce here."

She began sipping the water instead, though it was hard to moderate herself when it tasted so delicious.

The shaggy-haired man said, "You will be treated—"

"One of our party is injured and requires medical care," interrupted Carina.

"We know," he replied. "Someone is coming to attend to her as we speak. As I was saying, you'll be treated well while you're here. Perhaps contrary to what you've heard, we don't torture, rape, or kill skydwellers. I know you've had a hard journey through the forest, but that was unavoidable. We have no way of traversing it except for walking. Now you can eat, rest, and wait. When your ransom is paid, you can return to Japheth."

"What are you talking about?" asked Carina. "What ransom?"

He smiled. "You know the score. You've had an unfortunate accident and ended up in our domain. In return for rescuing you and keeping you safe while you're here, we require a reward."

"Rescuing us?" Carina said. "We didn't need rescuing, and we certainly didn't need ropes tied around our necks or being forced to march for hours."

"The jungle isn't safe, especially not at night," said the man. "If our hunting party hadn't been nearby when you crashed, you wouldn't have survived until morning. Some forest predators are drawn by the sound of human voices, for instance. I apologize if you were roughly treated, but it was for your own safety."

"For our own safety?" Carina asked bitterly. "I'd hate to find out what you do to people you *aren't* trying to keep safe. Look, I get what's going on here. You think we're from Japheth, and you plan on extorting money from our friends and relations in exchange for our return. It sounds like some kind of local custom. Well, you're wrong. We aren't from Japheth and we aren't even Magogian. We're offworlders, and now you've brought us where we planned on going anyway, we're going to thank you and leave."

She managed to rise halfway to her feet before one of the hunters clamped a hand on her shoulder and forced her down.

"So much for hospitality," she muttered.

35

B ryce looked down at Jace as he lay in bed in his cabin, recovering from his ordeal. After they'd talked only a short while, the mage had suddenly fallen asleep. He looked calm and relaxed, and Bryce was glad.

He didn't think he'd ever forget the sight of Jace as he was carried from the cabin where the Lotacryllans had kept him. Rebane had tortured the poor man cruelly and must have persisted until the last minute in trying to force him to open the armory. Jace had been covered in cuts, some still fresh and dripping blood.

In his own way, the mage had been the most heroic of all who had fought to rid the *Bathsheba* of the menace of mutiny. He'd allowed himself to be taken hostage, and he'd endured excruciating pain and the threat of death in order to weigh the battle heavily in favor of the Black Dogs.

His heroism had continued even after his rescue by Jackson's team, which had entered Deck Three through the airlock. Now that the battle was over, Bryce had been about to comm Ferne or Oriana to ask them to Heal Jace. Even though the man's appearance was gruesome, he'd thought it was a better alternative to treatment by the medics, who had feared they might not save him. But Jace had asked for elixir and set about Healing himself.

Bryce gazed at the sleeping man for another few moments to reassure himself he really was okay, and then left the cabin. There was still plenty to do in the post-battle cleanup.

He comm'd Jackson and asked the merc to meet him on the bridge.

By the time he arrived, Jackson was already there, along with Gulay and two more long-serving members of the Black Dogs: Van Hasty and Rees. The four had become unofficial leaders of the band in Carina's absence. As he had himself, Bryce reflected. Who could have known so much would happen aboard the ship while Carina was gone buying fuel?

As he thought of her, he realized he hadn't heard from her in a while—longer than he would have anticipated. She'd said she didn't trust the man who was playing host to them. Disquiet niggled at him as he found an empty seat and sat down. He hoped she was okay. If the fuel purchase had gone smoothly, they should be back soon.

After making a mental note to comm Carina for an update soon, he said to the assembled Black Dogs, "So, have you come to a decision?"

One important question had been pressing ever since they'd crushed the Lotacryllans' mutiny: what should they do with the enemy survivors?

"We're at a stalemate," Jackson replied.

"Let me guess," Bryce said, "*you* think we should execute them rather than maroon them."

The merc gave a short, sharp nod. "Gulay agrees with me. Even if we could overlook the mutiny, after what they did to the mage, they don't deserve to live."

"*They* didn't do it, though, did they?" said Van Hasty. The woman's cheek was purple and swollen, and she still hadn't changed out of her armor. "It was Rebane, and he's already paid for it. Too quickly, but that can't be helped now."

"But none of them tried to stop him, did they?" Gulay asked.

"We don't know that," Rees countered. He'd had several teeth knocked out in the battle. A medic had filled the space with synthetic enamel to serve as a temporary replacement while his new teeth were grown. "They could have argued with him about it, tried to reason him out of it. We just don't know."

"If it was me," said Jackson, "I wouldn't have tried to 'reason him out of it', I would have cut off his fucking hands."

"Whether they agreed to the torture or not, they went along with the mutiny," Gulay pointed out, "even though we saved them from the Regians. You can't argue with that."

Van Hasty gingerly prodded her bruise. "I don't know. It's one thing to kill the enemy in battle, but killing them in cold blood? Doesn't feel good."

"Let's not forget," said Bryce, "we aren't only talking about what the Lotacryllans might or might not deserve. We also have to think about the repercussions of whatever decision we make. If we only maroon them, there's a chance they could be rescued and come after us for revenge."

"And if we execute them," Rees said, "*more* Lotacryllans could come after us for revenge."

"I don't think that's very likely," said Gulay. "Lomang and Mezban are dead, and we're months, maybe years, from their planet. How would they even find out what we'd done?"

"Rebane might have got a comm off, updating them on the situation," Bryce said, ruing his omission in not checking what messages were leaving the ship.

"Still, that place is many light years away," Gulay replied. "By the time the Lotacryllans got here, we'd be long gone. One of the kids could do that thing where they cover the engine's trace."

"Talking of which," said Jackson, "where's our fuel? Why isn't Carina back yet?"

"That's another story," Bryce replied, "too long to tell right now. The last time I heard from her, they were all okay. Hopefully, they'll be back soon."

"She's going to have the shock of her life finding half the ship's company gone," Jackson said.

"We haven't decided for sure we're going to execute them," said Rees irritably.

Jackson threw up his hands. "I've had enough of this. We're going around in circles." He stood up. "If you decide to space them, let me know. I want to be there to see them go out the airlock. Especially that big bastard." He strode across the bridge and stepped through the open doorway.

When he was out of sight, Van Hasty asked cheekily, "Does that mean his vote doesn't count?"

Bryce rolled his eyes. "No, it doesn't."

Once more, he had the deciding vote. This time, he felt more confident about it. His instinct that the Lotacryllans were planning a mutiny had been correct. He hoped he would make the right decision this time, too.

Execute or maroon?

Van Hasty had been right—the idea of killing someone who wasn't actively trying to kill you didn't feel good. The fact that he didn't know to what extent the Lotacryllans had been persuaded by Rebane made it worse. It could be that, in other circumstances and under the influence of a different leader, the bearded men could have been friends.

On the other hand, they'd spat in the face of the people who had helped them and turned a blind eye to torture.

There had to be a point at which the bearded men should be held responsible for their actions and forced to face the consequences.

THEY LINED them up in the passageway.

Bryce stood at the airlock, determined to look each man in the eye. He'd delayed making a decision on what would happen to them until after the quiet shift, which had led to a sleepless night. Then, when he'd gotten out of bed, he still hadn't made up his mind.

In the end, he'd come down to practicalities. Whether or not the Lotacryllans deserved to die for what they'd done, for pure safety's sake he couldn't let them live. Gulay had been right—the chances that anyone else might find out they'd been executed were tiny, but if they remained alive, they would be a constant, though remote, threat.

The bearded men reacted to their imminent death in different ways. Some pleaded for their lives on their knees, and had to be dragged into the airlock. Jackson wanted to shoot these ones in the head on the spot, but to Bryce that seemed somehow more barbaric. Recoiling from a vision of bodies oozing blood and brain matter among the soon-to-be executed, he told him, no, every one of them had to be spaced.

Other Lotacryllans hung their heads and shuffled in, as if only obeying yet another order, though a somewhat unpleasant one. A few fought ferociously. It was clear to all present that there was no way they could win, that their fate was inevitable, but they fought anyway. Pappu was among these. He roared and raged, throwing his massive arms around, shackled at the wrists. He must have been in great pain as no Black Dog medic had treated his wounds. In the end, Jackson stunned him, and four mercs were required to drag his bulk to the airlock.

It was the ones who fought that gave Bryce the most pain, not because he felt any deep pity or sympathy for them, but because they reminded him of Carina. She fell into the camp of people who would fight until the last breath left their bodies.

Finally, the job was done.

Like his memory of Jace after his torture, Bryce knew it would be a long time before he forgot the view through the airlock window of the outer door opening and the bearded men drifting away, asphyxiating, agonized by ruptured lungs, sprays of their blood freezing instantly in space.

The Black Dogs left, and the passageway was empty. Bryce remained there for a long time, alone with his thoughts, until he also left.

He went to visit the twins and Nahla, hoping their wholesomeness might help heal his soul.

36

The man with the damaged arm was called Patrin. Carina spun him a tale about how they were tourists who had rented a glider for sightseeing and had crashed. She didn't think he believed her, but, true to his word, he provided them with food, water, and a comfortable place to sleep, as well as medical treatment for Hsiao and also for Justus, whose hands were bloodied and blistered from hauling the pilot's litter.

Though they were being treated reasonably well, they weren't free to leave. The ground-dwelling Magogians put them in a hut with two guards while they decided what to do with them. Whatever the decision was, Carina was confident it wouldn't work in her or her companions' favor. Nor would their captors react well to any escape attempts, of that she was certain.

While their captors had attended to their needs, it had begun to rain again. The drops drummed heavily on the roof of their hut, and the humidity, which had been more bearable now they were on the coast, noticeably increased. Conditions under cover were close, almost stifling, and Carina was wet with sweat.

Their plan to buy starship fuel on Magog was in tatters. The planet was no longer anything more than a dangerous place to stick around. Kai Wei's disappearance had to have been noticed by now, and records would probably show they were involved in it somehow.

They had to make elixir so Darius could Send to Poppy. Once they were safe inside the starwhale, they could figure out what to do next. Unfortunately, the hunting party had removed everyone's ear comm, so they had no way to update their companions on the *Bathsheba* about what had happened.

Mattresses filled with some kind of dried plants had been placed around the inside walls of their windowless hut, and at the center sat a glowing globe. The bowls and platters from their meal had been removed by the guards, and they'd been left with a large container of water and cups in case they were thirsty overnight.

As soon as the last Magogian left and the hut door had been locked, Carina walked over to it and pressed her ear against it. No sounds from the village penetrated. Next, she went to the globe in the center of the room and tentatively touched its surface. It was slightly cool, not hot or even warm as she'd expected it to be. She picked it up. Aside from a ring around the base that it stood upon, the lamp bore no other markings.

"Solar-powered?" Justus offered from his corner of the hut, where he sat upon a mattress, one knee raised and his other leg stretched out.

"I guess it must be something like that," Carina replied. "It's a pity. If we could make a fire, we might not even need to escape. Or, at least, not until Poppy gets here. Then she might scare our Magogian friends so much they run off." She picked up one of the cups and looked at it thoughtfully.

"Do you have all the ingredients with you?" asked Parthenia, hugging her knees.

"I do. You still have your canister, right?"

Parthenia pulled the metal container out from a deep pocket in her pajama pants. She'd been wearing the yellow clothes ever since Carina had woken her up at Wei's mansion, though they were much the worse for wear now, covered in dirt and ripped in several places.

All they needed was a fire, and Carina knew exactly where one was. She wouldn't even have to try to make one with a firestone. But scores of Magogians lay between her and the central village hearth. And they would have only one chance at escape. If they failed, they would be locked up much more securely afterward.

Hsiao was lying down but awake.

"How are you feeling?" Carina asked her.

"A lot better," replied the pilot. "Their doctor gave me something that really pepped me up."

"We might need to run," said Carina.

"I know. I think I'm up to it."

"I'll carry the little one, if necessary," said Justus.

Darius was already asleep.

Carina nodded. "We have a few hours to wait before we can make our move. I want to leave about an hour before dawn. But we have plenty to do in the meantime."

"Do you have a plan for getting us out?" Hsiao asked.

Carina held up the cup.

THE OBVIOUS WAY TO escape would have been to make a commotion to attract the guards' attention, and then when they unlocked the door, to jump them, knock them out, and run. Only that would entail making a lot of noise, and, in the village environment, they wouldn't just attract the attention of the guards. The entire village would be after them, and they would be caught and returned to their comfortable prison within minutes.

Carina's plan took more time and effort, but it was much quieter.

She sat back on her haunches, wiped her hair from her sweaty brow with the back of her forearm, and surveyed the results of their efforts. The hole looked to be around a meter and a half deep. They'd reached the bottom of the wall of the hut and dug underneath it as well as a considerable distance up the other side. Piles of sand filled the space around their excavation.

If they'd had something bigger than cups to dig with, they would have been able to finish their work much quicker. Digging out the soft sand floor was easy, though the sand regularly collapsed into the hole. But only being able to remove cupfuls at a time lengthened the process, even with everyone except Darius digging at once.

"Once we break through on the other side," Carina said, "we'll have to move fast. We can't risk someone wandering past on a nighttime visit to the latrine and falling in our hole."

"When we get close to the surface, the sand will collapse and make our job a lot easier," said Justus.

"Ugh," Parthenia murmured. "I am *not* looking forward to crawling through that."

"Is it time to wake up Darius?" Hsiao asked.

He'd slept through the entire day and night of digging.

"Yeah," Carina replied. "He needs to know what's going on before we leave."

Parthenia left her position next to the hole and crossed the hut to Darius.

While her sister was waking their brother, Carina climbed

into the hole, squatted down, and reached under the base of the wooden wall to scrape sand from the far side.

Soon after she resumed work, an avalanche of sand descended on her arm and spilled over the floor of the hole.

"Let me do it," said Justus.

Carina climbed out to allow the large man to take her place.

He set to work with his bandaged hands, scooping out the loose material at a fast pace.

"We must force our way through," he said breathlessly after a few minutes' work. "The sand is looser on the other side. It will never stop falling in. I will go first. When each of you reaches the other side, put up your hand. I will pull you out."

He bent forward and pushed his head through the remaining narrow space under the planks that formed the wall. Bracing himself with his feet, he wriggled forward, easing his wide shoulders under the wall before bringing his arms forward.

Sand spilled out as he swept it behind him. Gradually, his torso disappeared, and then his hips.

Carina couldn't imagine how he was breathing as he moved through to the other side.

Justus's thighs slid under the wall, and then his knees and calves. Finally, his feet glided out of sight. Two long grooves in the sand were all that remained of his presence.

"Who's next?" Carina asked.

"I'll do it," said Hsiao. "It shouldn't be hard following in Justus's wake."

As the pilot climbed into the depression, Carina turned to check on Darius. Her brother's eyes were only half open, but he looked ready to go. Parthenia, however, looked scared.

"What's the matter?" Carina asked her.

Her sister's gaze flicked to meet hers before she looked away again. "Isn't there another way we can do this?"

"It's a little late to talk about it now, but, no, I don't think there is. Is something wrong?"

"I just hate the thought of crawling through that sand."

On a closer inspection, Carina saw Parthenia was sweating. She had to be really scared.

"It's okay," Darius piped up. "You'll be fine."

Carina reached out and touched her sister's arm. "I'm sorry, but we have to do this."

"I know," she replied shakily. "It's only...I wish we didn't."

"I'll tell you what we'll do," Carina said. "Let's go through together."

Parthenia gave a small smile. "I'd like that."

37

Carina half expected to be immediately apprehended by the villagers as she climbed out of the hole, but when she emerged into the refreshingly cool air outdoors, Justus heaving her out with one arm and dragging up Parthenia with the other, she found only the Lotacryllan, Hsiao, and Darius waiting for them. Her brother had wriggled his way to the other side efficiently, and seemed to find the enterprise a lot of fun.

Night had not yet left that part of Magog, she was relieved to see. And the stars were out. Slipping away into the forest should be fairly easy.

They were nearly on their way...if not home, then on to the next stage of their journey. Magog had turned out not to be an unexpected sanctuary after all, but Earth still remained somewhere out in the black, and as long as it did, hope for a better life for her and her family remained, too.

"Which way do we go?" Hsiao asked in a barely audible whisper.

Their hut was located at the edge of the village, and they were standing behind it. Thirty meters or so distant lay the ocean's edge. To reach the jungle they had to go around the village's outskirts.

Or directly through it.

"You all go that way," Carina said, pointing to her right. "I'll meet you in the forest."

"Where are *you* going?" asked Justus.

"I'm hoping the villagers keep their fire burning day and night. I'm going to—"

"That's crazy!" Parthenia interjected.

"Yesterday's rainstorm will have soaked every piece of wood not under cover," Carina explained. "I want to—"

"I know what you want to do," Parthenia interrupted again. "You're going to try to take some sticks from the fire. It's too risky. We should be focusing on escaping. We can make a fire later, when we're far away from here."

"We won't have time," Carina argued. "It'll be daylight soon, and the guards will check on us. The instant they see we're gone, that guy Patrin will send hunters after us. They'll track us through the jungle in no time. Tracking is what they do."

Parthenia's features fell.

"We have to move *fast*," Carina continued, "if Poppy is to reach us before the hunters do."

The others agreed, telling Parthenia to come with them. They set off, and Carina went with them for a short distance in order to avoid the guards she guessed were standing outside their hut. Then she left the group, slipping between two dwellings, and began to move toward the village's center. She kept to the pitch black shadows cast by the low buildings in the starlight.

Everyone in the village seemed to be asleep. As Carina walked softly past one hut she heard a deep, rumbling snore. If her luck held out, she would be able to grab the cool end of two or three large, burning sticks and run out to the jungle within a couple of minutes.

The sight of a patch of glowing red made her heart thump. She was right. The villagers did keep a fire going. They must have covered it with a metal sheet or something during the storm.

She'd reached the open space in the center. Poking her head out, she saw no one about.

Her heart in her mouth, she tiptoed toward the fire.

All was silent in the Magogian village.

Parthenia, Darius, and the others must have reached the jungle by now.

Carina felt the heat from the gleaming embers. She knelt down for a closer look. There were usually a few unburned ends of wood protruding from a regular wood fire.

She saw one.

Reaching out, she picked it up. The other end of the stick spurted flame as she moved it.

Was there another?

Suddenly, the doors of the surrounding huts opened, and Magogians poured out.

Carina dropped the stick as if she'd been holding the burning end. She leapt up and spun around, looking for a gap in the mob that was descending on her.

There was none.

Before she could even take a step, the first of the villagers had reached her, grabbed her by the waist, and thrown her onto the sand.

"Mage!" the man shouted. "Filthy mage! I knew that's what you were all along."

Dumbfounded, Carina could only stare up at him.

More men and women arrived. One woman kicked Carina's side. A man spat at her.

"Okay, calm down, calm down," said a familiar voice.

Patrin had arrived.

With his good arm, he pushed the villagers back and they obeyed, though sullenly.

Leaning over Carina, he said, "I'm sorry. I wish things could be different, but you've sealed your own fate."

Then he moved back and motioned to two men in the crowd, who came forward and picked her up.

At the same time, someone shouted from farther away, among the huts, "We've got them!"

Still too surprised and confused even to struggle, Carina looked in the direction of the voice and was dismayed to see her companions approaching, pushed forward by villagers who had caught them.

The sight sparked her into anger that swept away her befuddlement. Fighting the grasp of the men holding her, she swung around to face Patrin. "What's going on?! What did that man call me? What are you going to do to us?"

The village leader stepped closer to her. "We suspected what you are, and when you went for the fire, you confirmed it. We have rules about what we do with skydwellers. Ordinary people, we return—for a price. But not mages. Your kind are evil, and you've done us great harm for many centuries. If a mage falls to the ground and ends up in our village, he or she never leaves it alive."

He turned away and called out, "Bind them! Take them down to the water. The tide rises in half an hour."

38

D awn was approaching as the Magogians forced Carina and her companions down to the ocean's edge. The stars in the east had faded in the paling sky, and at the horizon a patch of rosy light signaled the imminent arrival of the sun.

Her wrists bound tightly behind her back, and pushed forward at a pace that made her trip and stumble in the loose sand, Carina struggled to believe that what was happening was real.

Was she really living her last moments?

Behind her, she could hear the villagers bringing the rest of her party down to the water.

Were they all about to die?

Even Parthenia?

Even *Darius*?!

Patrin was walking ahead of her, striding fast, as if he wanted to get the job over quickly.

"Hey!" Carina shouted. "Hey, Patrin! Tell me what's going on. I don't understand."

The man didn't answer or break pace.

They'd nearly reached the wet sand, where the waves had lapped hours before. Now, the tide was low, and a little farther out flat stones protruded from the beach. Carina saw things fixed to them, though she couldn't make out what they were in the predawn light.

A short distance beyond the stones, a line of shallow waves rose and fell.

"Patrin!" Carina yelled again. "Answer me! I told you we're offworlders. We don't have anything to do with Magogian conflicts. You've got us mixed up with some other group. Whatever you're planning, it's wrong. We've never done anything to harm your people!"

Still, he refused to even acknowledge her.

Carina began to despair. How could she get through to him?

They drew closer to the stones, and suddenly she could see what was attached to them: chains and manacles.

The villagers were going to chain them to the rocks, and when the tide came in they would drown.

"*No!*"

She fought against the grip of the man who was holding her bound wrists.

"NO! Let me go!"

But the Magogian's hold on her was iron-strong.

"Why are you *doing* this?!"

They'd reached one of the stones. Sea water was already seeping around its base at each wash of waves on the shore.

Carina stared at the chains. Thick links interwoven, covered in rust and crustaceans, they lay forlorn on the rock surface.

How many had died in their grasp?

"Patrin!!" Carina screamed.

The man had stopped and was standing between the stones, his good hand on his hip while his other arm hung loosely. He wouldn't meet her gaze.

In her desperation, she switched tactics.

"Patrin," she said more quietly, the sea breeze whipping her hair across her lips. "Please. My brother is seven. He's only seven years old." Tears filled her eyes, and her throat was so tight she could hardly speak. "He's never hurt anyone in his life. How can you do this to a child? He's just a little boy."

Her words seemed to have an effect. The village leader's blank expression faltered, and he looked away from her.

A little way down the beach, her companions had also reached the flat rocks. Parthenia was crying, while Hsiao and Justus seemed to be in a state of shock. Darius didn't appear to understand what was happening. He was looking at Carina with puzzlement in his eyes.

The man who was holding her let go of her wrists, and a second later, her bindings were cut. He pushed her onto the rock, and she fell, her kneecaps smacking into the stone.

She could try and fight her captor, but she couldn't fight all the Magogians. If she managed to get away, she would have to leave her companions to die.

"Please don't hurt my brother," she begged Patrin. "Please. He's only a kid. I thought you were better than that. I can't believe you would be so cruel. Why would you do this to a young boy?"

The leader's shoulders sagged and his features took on a pained look.

He pointed at the man who was holding Darius. "Release him and take him back to the village."

The tears in Carina's eyes flooded down her cheeks. "Thank you."

"One of our families will take him in and bring him up," Patrin said. "He will never return to the sky or know what he is."

Carina was pushed onto her back, and her captor put a foot on her stomach to hold her down. He lifted a manacle and worked at it, forcing open the rusty hinges.

She decided the time for dissembling was gone. If he was going to spare their lives, she had to convince him they had nothing to do with the mages who lived in the cloud cities, who seemed to have done the ground-dwelling Magogians a lot of harm.

"Okay," she said. "I admit it. I am a mage. How did you know?"

A squeak sounded above her. The man trying to open the manacle had succeeded. He pushed it under her wrist and closed it.

"For stars' sake," Carina exclaimed when Patrin didn't answer, "I'm about to die. What harm can it do to tell me how you guessed what I am?"

Patrin regarded her with a sullen, angry gaze. "There were no injuries. When our hunting party found the wreckage of your glider, they saw one man had died, but when they caught up to the survivors, none of you had any injuries. That was strange after such a serious crash.

"We know mages can heal using magic. It is one of the many pieces of information about your kind we've gathered over the years. We also know that to cast your spells you must drink a special liquid, which you brew over a fire. The hunters found no liquid on your persons, so I thought if you were mages you would try to make some as soon as you escaped. I *allowed* you to escape in order to watch your behavior. When you tried to steal some fire, that was when I knew for sure what you are."

As Patrin had been speaking, Carina's captor had fastened a manacle around her other wrist and was now working on the ones near her ankles. Waves were splashing against his calves and over the rock. Cold water was soaking her legs.

"You're right," she admitted. "You were absolutely right in your guesses. But you're wrong about one thing: we aren't from Magog. We have nothing to do with the mages here.

Where I come from, mages live in secret and fear. I don't know exactly what they do here, but the reason we crashed in the glider was because we were trying to get *away* from a mage. We knew he was evil, and we didn't want anything to do with him."

Patrin's face had resumed its blank expression. Carina was sure he felt bad about what he was doing, but he was trying to shut down his guilty feelings and empathy for them. If she could only think of one convincing point to support what she was saying, she might tip him into changing his mind.

Both her ankles were now fastened to the rock. The man had closed the manacles and stepped aside.

A large wave arrived and splashed up her body, temporarily covering her face in water. She coughed out the harsh salt water that had run up her nose.

She was cold, shivering from the sudden deluge of chilly water. How much longer did she have until the waves entirely covered her? How long would she hold her breath, refusing to succumb to the inevitable?

Her thoughts turned to Hsiao and Justus, who were not even mages. She'd asked them to come along on the trip, and now they were going to die. They'd been loyal and helpful companions and as a result they would lose their lives, like Halliday and Kamil.

She remembered what Calvaley had told her: *People will die under your command. It is inevitable. Yet you must make whatever decisions you have to make and live without regret.*

She couldn't do it. She would spend these last remaining minutes of her life in bitter regret.

And Parthenia. She was so young, and not at all to blame for anything that had happened.

She wanted to talk to her sister and try to offer her some words of comfort, something to try to ease the pain, but she couldn't see her. All she could see was the brightening morning sky and Patrin, off to one side. The man who had fastened her manacles had left.

Poor Parthenia, still in her yellow pajamas.

Her yellow pajamas!

Patrin moved as if to leave.

"Wait!" Carina gasped. "Wait! If I can prove to you we aren't from Magog, will you at least let me explain how mages from other places aren't evil?"

A second large wave rose and fell, inundating her. She held her breath until the water drained away.

Patrin had stopped and was watching her, waiting for her to speak.

"Look at our clothes. Do they look like the clothes of people who live in Japheth? I mean, mine and Hsiao's and Justus's. My sister, Parthenia, she's wearing night clothes she was given by the Magogian mage I told you about. Look how expensive they are compared to ours. Ours were printed on a starship. They're rougher, coarser, and nowhere near so fine or fancy."

Carina wasn't at all confident that the quality of Parthenia's pajamas was still evident after their trek through the jungle, but it was all the evidence she could muster.

A third wave hit.

This time, it seemed to take an age to retreat. When Carina's head finally appeared from the water, she gasped for air.

Patrin said, "I will give you the opportunity to tell your story. It had better be a good one."

39

No one spoke a word as they trudged up the beach. Carina risked a glance back at the flat stones, but they were gone, entirely covered by waves. She gave a shudder that had only a little to do with her sodden, cold clothes and wet hair cooling in the sea breeze.

Except for Darius, they had all come within minutes of dying, and they were not safe yet, not by a long shot. She would tell Patrin about her life and answer all his questions truthfully.

Whether he would believe her was another matter.

At the very least, she would buy them another few hours of life. And in that time their fortunes might change. A lot could happen in a few hours.

By the time they reached the village, she was shaking.

Patrin led them and the people guarding them to the central hearth. The villagers spread some blankets, and one of them thrust another at Carina. She wrapped it around her shoulders and sat down in the spot the leader indicated.

Darius sat down next to her, and she opened her blanket to wrap it around both of them. Her brother didn't ask her what was going on. If he didn't know, he could sense the seriousness of the situation.

Another villager approached to offer her a steaming cup of the local drink. She took it, profoundly grateful for the kindness. The ground-dwelling Magogians were good people. She couldn't imagine what the mages in the cloud cities had done to them to make them behave so harshly in retaliation.

She sipped the hot drink as the others sat down, and then, after blowing on it, passed it to Darius.

Patrin crossed his legs and sat opposite her, his eyes grave. "Begin."

Carina took a breath and looked up at the bright blue sky. Where to start?

She decided to go right back to her earliest memories, of Ma and Ba's disappearance, and go on from there. As long as she talked, she and her companions would remain alive.

So she told him everything, all about what her life had been like growing up, about becoming a merc and rescuing Darius without knowing he was her half-brother. Then she told him how she'd been reunited with her mother, though in terrible circumstances, and discovered she had a whole family of half-siblings as well as her little brother. She explained that she'd helped them escape from slavery, and her mother had died, and that they were now trying to reach their origin planet in the hope they could live there free from persecution and danger. She also told Patrin about Castiel, about how he was a different kind of mage, and all the cruel and evil things he'd done.

The telling of her story took a long time, and as she neared the end, yet another Magogian day had sped past. The sun was beginning to set, Carina's clothes had dried on her, stiff with salt, and her hair was dry and tacky, plastered to her head.

"We came to Magog to buy starship fuel," she said.

Then she gasped and reached for her pocket.

"What's wrong?" asked Patrin.

His demeanor had altered as he'd listened, turning friendlier and more relaxed.

Her fingers touched a small, lumpy bundle distorting the outline of her pants. She sighed with relief, though she knew they were not safe yet. Continuing in the spirit of complete honesty, she pulled out the pouch of ember gems and opened it.

"I thought I might have lost these," she said, tipping out the gems into her hand and then holding them out for Patrin to see. "I thought they might have been washed out in the waves."

He took one and held it up. The lowering sun's beams were captured in the jewel and flashed them out again, doubling the stone's interior fire. "Beautiful."

"They're very rare and very valuable," Carina said. "You could have them all if you would let us go. Or maybe, let us keep just one. We still need to buy fuel."

Patrin cocked an eyebrow. "Why would I need you to give them to me? I could easily take them."

Carina had no reply to offer. He was entirely right.

After an awkward pause, the leader laughed. "I'm only kidding with you. We aren't thieves, though these would make an excellent reward for returning you to Japheth."

"But we aren't—"

"I know. I'm kidding again." Patrin's features turned more serious. "I believe you. No one could make up a story like that on the spot, especially not one so long." He turned to the onlookers. "My butt's gone numb from sitting here listening."

The Magogian villagers laughed, and so did Carina, though uneasily. She hoped she really had convinced him of the truth of what she'd said.

Patrin dropped the gem he'd been holding into the pouch before folding her fingers over it. "Keep them."

The gesture finally reassured her they were no longer in any danger. She almost wept with relief.

The leader stood up and stretched. "We all need a break. And you need a shower and clean clothes. Then we'll talk about what you do next."

Carina rose awkwardly to her feet, gently pulling Darius up with her. A woman approached and told them to follow her. She led them to a set of cubicles on the village outskirts. Walls made from woven plant material provided privacy around plain showers on concrete bases. The water wasn't heated, but it was warm from the tank sitting in the sun all day.

She washed the salt from her skin with a bar of handmade soap and used the same soap to wash her hair. When she emerged, she put on clothes the villagers had prepared for her. Her old, dirty clothes were piled next to them.

The others were waiting, except for Darius, who skipped out to join them a few minutes later. When they were all ready, they were led back to the center of the village.

Patrin was already there, in the same spot near the fire, silhouetted by the flames in the darkness. Most of the other villagers had left and only the crackle of the burning wood and wind in the forest trees disturbed the quiet.

Carina sat down, and the leader said, "I want to thank you for telling me your story today."

"No problem. It was my pleasure, considering I was trying to save all our lives."

"That's why I'm thanking you. If we'd executed you, we would have done a great wrong, without even knowing it."

"From what you've said, your people have suffered a lot at the hands of the mages in the cloud cities."

Patrin heaved a sigh. "You've only been here a short time, so it's understandable you don't know anything about it, but the skydwellers have kept us crushed and subjugated for many generations. Here in Japheth District things aren't as bad as they are in other areas of Magog. We aren't forced to work in factories in appalling conditions just to eat. But, look around. You see how we live. We're kept at subsistence level, hunting in the forest or farming the ocean for food. We aren't allowed access to any of the technologies the skydwellers have at their disposal.

"They tell us their machines and devices are too complex for us to understand; that there's a fundamental difference in mental capacity between people who live on the ground compared to those born at higher altitudes. They promote this myth and use it as an excuse to keep us down and deny us the basic freedoms they enjoy."

"That's disgusting," said Carina. "I guess there isn't much you can do about it, not when the cloud cities are so inaccessible."

"There have been many attempts at rebellion over the years. People sneaking aboard the massive factory transports that deliver goods to cities, sabotaging their tethers, or even attempting to climb up them. All were unsuccessful. We have knives, spears, and bows and arrows, they have guns— imported from offplanet. They would never trust us to manufacture weapons."

Though she wasn't sure she wanted to hear the answer, a question was burning in Carina's mind. "I can understand your animosity toward skydwellers, but why do you hate the mages so much in particular? What have they done?"

Patrin passed his hand over his eyes. "Whenever there's a rebellion, or any attempt to stand up to the skydwellers, it's the mages who give the punishment. Every city contains tall, white towers. Some are straight and some are twisted, but they all serve the same purpose: they are death chambers for rebels. The mages take them and they move them inside the towers by magic."

"I remember them," said Parthenia. "I saw them in the

distance from the spaceport. But, why do the mages Transport the rebels into the towers? Why not just walk them inside?"

Carina remembered the small-scale version of a white tower she'd seen in Kai Wei's garden. "Because they have no doors or windows."

Parthenia gasped and clapped a hand to her mouth. "They entomb them alive?"

The question needed no answer.

Patrin hung his head, and the group sat in silence.

Finally, Carina said, "I can see why you wanted to kill us."

"It would have been a quicker and more merciful death than your people suffer," said Justus.

"But it would have been a great injustice to inflict it on you," Patrin said. "I'm glad to hear that not all mages are evil."

"Very few mages are evil," said Carina. "I've only ever known one other. I don't understand why there are so many Dark Mages here."

"Maybe they aren't all Dark," Parthenia offered. "Maybe only one or two are like Wei, and they turn the others bad, or they trick them into doing evil things."

"Yeah, maybe. He certainly wanted to control us. He didn't like it when I saw through his Semblance."

"All this mage talk is very interesting," said Hsiao, "but some of us non-mages would like to get back to the *Bathsheba*, and we haven't completed our errand yet."

"Shoot," Carina said. "We have to leave, Patrin. I mean, it's been fun and all, but we have to go."

He chuckled. "I'm glad you've had a good time."

But, in the end, they didn't leave immediately. First, they had to brew elixir. Then, after Darius had Sent to Poppy and they were waiting for her to arrive, Carina, Parthenia, and Darius went about the village making whatever Casts they could to improve the lives of the villagers. They Healed those with medical complaints, Transported lumber felled in the forest to desired destinations, and then Split it into planks for huts.

Finally, when Poppy had landed on the beach and the villagers had assembled to say farewell, Carina pulled the pouch out of her pocket and opened it.

"I'm not sure how you can use these," she said to Patrin, removing three gems, "but I want to make a donation to the next rebellion."

She tried to give him the stones, but he shook his head. "I can't accept them. It's very generous of you, but no. They're too valuable, and, like you said, how would we use them?"

"You know, I believe you have our ear comms? Could you contact a ship delivering weapons from offplanet, and offer the captain a gem in payment? Just a suggestion. I have it on good authority that the person in charge of imports and exports is out of action for the foreseeable future."

Patrin looked thoughtful for a moment, then, with a smile, he held out his hand.

40

The starship fuel arrived at the *Bathsheba* via a hauler from Gog. Carina sat behind the transparent screen of one of Poppy's 'eyes', watching as the hauler transferred the fuel to the ship's tanks.

Her experience of buying fuel from a Gogian supplier had been absurdly easy compared to the terrible events she and her companions had endured on Magog. The smaller, much less populous world offered an easily accessible network offplanet visitors could connect to before arrival. Carina had made the arrangements via comm and had spent a total of about twenty minutes on the surface, purely in order to pay for her purchase.

She smiled as she recalled the fuel company owner's sardonic laugh when she'd told him they'd tried to buy fuel on Magog, without success.

"You went to Magog? How did you find it?" he asked sarcastically. "Did you like the people?"

As Carina struggled to find words to reply, he continued, "They're a bunch of crazies, right? Why do you think I live here on Gog? I'd rather live under a dome in a frozen desert than spend a day on Magog. What a load of lunatics."

Looking beyond the spaceport's transparent walls to the bare, rocky landscape and its scarce, tough, scrubby plants clinging to life in the inhospitable environment, she'd been inclined to agree. She, too, would rather have lived in that barren, cold, lonely place than in one of Magog's airy cities in the clouds, rubbing shoulders with parasitic human life, or as a ground-dweller, enduring hothouse conditions, deprivation, and servitude.

She'd given the man two of the ember gems, thankful that he'd known what they were from her initial description. From the speed with which he'd pocketed them, she had a feeling she'd paid too much, but she didn't really care. All she wanted to do was to get back to the *Bathsheba* and prepare for the next part of the journey.

The diversion caused by the Regian's invasion of the ship had cost many lives and added months to their voyage. Hopefully, the final stage would progress smoothly and without danger, though considering the way things had gone so far, perhaps that was too much to hope for. Perhaps simply making it to Earth with no further loss of life was the best potential outcome.

After returning to Poppy, she'd asked her, through Darius, to lead the fuel hauler back to the *Bathsheba*. What the hauler's captain thought of following a living space creature through the Aberama 8 system, she didn't know, but she guessed he was probably bemused.

It would only be a matter of minutes before Poppy docked, and she would finally see Bryce again. She had so much to say to him, things that hadn't felt right saying over comm. She wanted to tell him how much she'd missed him, and how she felt about him. At some point, she would also have to tell him everything that had happened on Magog.

She'd left out the worst of it in her comm messages, though he knew Halliday and Kamil were no longer with them, so the danger they'd been in was clear. She would have to tell him how close they'd all come to dying, but the details could wait.

Bryce had also seemed to have been holding something back in his replies to her. He'd told her what Ferne, Oriana, and Nahla had been doing, and that there had been some shake ups aboard the ship, but he hadn't said exactly what had been going on. She guessed it hadn't been anything too serious. He would have told her if they'd been attacked, and what else could have happened to them out there in the black?

The hauler's snake-like delivery tube broke free from the *Bathsheba's* fuel port and concertinaed, reducing in length until it was a stubby protuberance on the side of the hauler, and the ship began to pull away.

That was it.

She'd done what she'd set out to do, though the realization gave her no satisfaction. If she'd only chosen Gog as the place to buy the fuel, they would have been back at the *Bathsheba* ages ago and Kamil and Halliday would still be alive. Her heart ached at the memory of the two deaths.

In spite of the eventual 'success' of her mission, in some ways she'd failed.

Darius popped up at the entrance to the narrow chamber. "Ferne says thanks for the fuel and how long will it be until we dock? He and Oriana have some new designs they want to model for us."

"Oh my word," she replied. "The twins have been making clothes all the time we've been gone? They're going to run the printers dry."

Gog had been such a basic outpost, the range of starship supplies they would have found on Magog hadn't been available. All they'd been able to buy was fuel.

Carina looked out into space. It was hard to tell Poppy's speed without instruments, and she'd slowed down to a gentle glide as they'd neared the *Bathsheba*.

"I guess we'll be there in about five minutes," she said.

"Cool. I'll tell him." Darius dropped out of sight.

The starwhales were still hanging about the ship, probably waiting for Poppy to return. Soon, it would be time to say goodbye to their space-faring friend. What a sad day that would be. Carina doubted they would ever see such an amazing creature again.

She stood up to climb out and follow her brother.

Bryce was waiting at the airlock. When the lock opened and everyone else stepped out, Carina hung back for a moment, watching him. He stood patiently, holding her with his gaze.

Parthenia and Darius ran to hug Nahla and the twins. Hsiao left the airlock with Justus, who looked about expectantly, rather puzzled. After a moment, Carina understood why. None of his Lotacryllan compatriots had come to greet him, which was odd. Several Black Dogs were there to meet Hsiao, including Jackson, whose features were understandably somber. He and Halliday had worked together from way back. The latter's absence from the returning party must have brought home to Jackson the fact that yet another of the 'old guard' was gone.

He appeared to spot Justus looking lost, and went over to speak to him. The two walked away, Jackson's arm over the Lotacryllan's shoulders.

Hsiao touched a bulkhead before departing with her fellow soldiers, as if glad to be back.

"Come on, Carina," Darius called out, his face lit with joy at being reunited with his siblings. "What are you waiting for?"

"I'll see you all at the cabin," she replied, "in a minute."

When everyone except Bryce had departed, Carina walked

into his arms. They silently held each other, and she sank into the serenity of being close to him again.

Then she broke away and peered into his eyes.

"What's wrong?" he asked.

"You look...different. Like you've changed somehow. What happened while I was away?"

"Um, the Lotacryllans are gone."

"*Gone*?! Where did they go, and *how*?"

"It's a long story. Come on, let's go in. The twins have prepared a fashion show to commemorate your return."

"A fashion show? Sounds like fun."

"Yeah...You should probably work a little more enthusiasm into your voice when you talk to them about it."

"Ha, I'll try."

"So, what's next?" Bryce asked.

"We get ready to set off for the last part of the voyage. We'll have to figure out a Deep Sleep rota. I'll ask the techs if they can rig up a system that will bring everyone out of stasis if the ship's attacked."

"Great idea. Something like that might have saved us from the Regians. Our numbers are so low now, if we have to fight again, we'll need every man and woman."

Carina rubbed her eyes as sudden exhaustion hit her.

"You look beat," said Bryce. "Do you want to skip the fashion show?"

"No, I bet they've worked really hard. I don't want to disappoint them."

"You'd do anything for those kids, wouldn't you?"

"Of course. And so would you. I only hope Earth proves to be a safe place for them to grow up."

Thanks for reading!

CARINA LIN'S STORY CONCLUDES IN 2021

Sign up to my reader group for an exclusive free copy of the Star Mage Saga prequel, *Star Mage Exile*, discounts on new releases, review crew invitations and other interesting stuff:

https://jjgreenauthor.com/free-books/

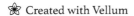

Printed in Great Britain
by Amazon